Who wants an Amish cowboy?

Annie liked a challenge. She th
situations. Tossing
shoulders, she plas
her prettiest smile.
a couple of my frien
mind you."

"Of course not," Levi agreed.

"And in return, I won't try and stop you from
talking to my family about moving to Texas."

"So now you're a matchmaker?"

"Think of me as a concerned bystander."

"All right. It's a deal." He held out his hand. "But
you have to shake on it."

But, just possibly, she'd found a way to keep her
life firmly rooted in Goshen, because she had
the perfect woman in mind for Levi Lapp and
this person would never consider moving away.

All Annie had to do was see to it that the two of
them fell in love. It would mean she'd have to
live around Levi the rest of her life…but at least
she wouldn't have to do so in Texas.

Vannetta Chapman has published over one hundred articles in Christian family magazines, receiving over two dozen awards from Romance Writers of America chapter groups. She discovered her love for the Amish while researching her grandfather's birthplace of Albion, Pennsylvania. Her first novel, *A Simple Amish Christmas*, quickly became a bestseller. Chapman lives in the Texas Hill Country with her husband.

Books by Vannetta Chapman

Love Inspired

Indiana Amish Brides

A Widow's Hope
Amish Christmas Memories
A Perfect Amish Match
The Amish Christmas Matchmaker

Visit the Author Profile page at Harlequin.com.

The Amish Christmas Matchmaker

Vannetta Chapman

Recycling programs
for this product may
not exist in your area.

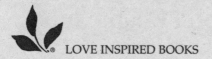

LOVE INSPIRED BOOKS

ISBN-13: 978-1-335-53945-8

The Amish Christmas Matchmaker

www.Harlequin.com

Printed in U.S.A.

Delight thyself also in the Lord:
and he shall give thee the desires of thine heart.
—*Psalm* 37:4

Thou shalt love thy neighbour as thyself.
There is none other commandment greater.
—*Mark* 12:31

This book is dedicated to Bob,
my very own cowboy.

Chapter One

Annie Kauffmann thought she'd just experienced a perfect day—business had gone well, the fall weather was exquisite and each member of her family was happy and healthy. She leaned her bicycle against the tree in the front yard and ran up the porch steps. Her mother was sitting in a rocker, knitting a baby blanket for her next grandchild. She had twelve and counting. If her mother was sitting, she was knitting—blankets, sweaters, caps and mittens.

"*Gut* day?" she asked.

"*Ya.*" Annie sank into a rocker, smoothing her apron over her dress and sinking back with a sigh. "I confirmed two more weddings."

"Your catering business is growing."

"It is. The *gut* thing about these is one is for December…"

"Not many winter weddings, so you must be speaking of Widow Schwartz."

"The same. The other is for later this month."

"You had an opening this month?"

"*Ya*, since you know… Jesse's was cancelled."

"Real shame that Emma changed her mind. I believe she'll regret that."

"Maybe not though, Mamm. Maybe not."

Annie was suddenly aware of voices in the house—her father and another man. She peeked out over the porch railing, wondering whose buggy she had missed, but there wasn't one there.

"Who is Dat talking to?"

"I believe his name is Levi."

"Levi King?"

"*Nein*. Levi Lapp."

"I don't know a Levi Lapp."

"He's new here."

"New?"

"Arrived yesterday."

"Did he walk?"

"I imagine he rode a bus to town, but he walked here today to see your *dat*."

"Who does he know in Goshen?"

"He's staying with Simon King."

"Is he related to Old Simon?"

"I'm not sure."

Now Annie's curiosity was thoroughly piqued.

"I think I need a glass of lemonade. Can I get you anything?"

Mamm smiled, not fooled for a minute. "Of course, dear. I would love that."

Annie stepped into the coolness of the house. Though it was September, the temperatures had remained warm, and the cool living room was a relief after her bike ride from town. Her father and Levi Lapp were in the kitchen, which would work perfectly. She straightened her apron, made sure her *kapp* wasn't askew and walked into the kitchen as if she had no idea she was interrupting.

She aimed for a casual stride but stumbled when she spied the man in a cowboy hat. A cowboy hat? She shook her head as if that would clear up what she was seeing.

"Annie. I'm glad you're home. I want you to meet Levi… Levi Lapp."

"Hello."

Levi tipped the cowboy hat, revealing blond hair that curled at his collar. "Howdy, ma'am."

Howdy, ma'am?

Had she fallen asleep and landed in a Western? "I'm Annie."

"It's nice to meet you."

"And you, as well. I was just fetching two glasses of lemonade. Don't let me interrupt…"

"Levi's from Pennsylvania—the Lancaster Plain community."

"*Ya?* I imagine it's cooler there." She didn't care about the weather in Pennsylvania, but she couldn't exactly ask about the hat.

"It was cooler when I left. Now Texas, where I plan to go, is still much warmer. They have days in the eighties right through November."

"Texas?" Annie had pulled two glasses from the cabinet. At the mention of Texas she turned toward Levi, holding the glasses and trying to remember what she was going to do with them.

He wasn't ugly exactly, only odd looking because of the hat. He seemed to be tall and on the thin side, had a healthy tan and broad shoulders. His blue eyes twinkled as if he understood her confusion and was enjoying it.

Annie raised her chin a fraction higher. "I wasn't aware there were Plain communities in Texas."

"Oh, *ya.* There's one in Beeville, which has been there nearly twenty years. Only a few families, though."

"And you're going there?" It was really none of her business. She placed the glasses on the counter and walked over to the propane-powered refrigerator. Removing the pitcher of lemonade, she held it up, but her *dat* waved her away, and Levi didn't seem to notice. A dreamy expression had come over his face. It was as if he'd been transported to another place. She'd seen that look before—usually on a man who was smitten with a girl.

"Not to Beeville, to Stephenville."

"But you said…"

"There's no community there now, but there was. It's where I grew up."

"You should hear the stories he tells, Annie." Her *dat* leaned back and crossed his arms. "Rolling hills, space for a family to grow, cattle and horses…"

Now she was noticing the starry look in her *dat*'s eyes. She'd seen that before. The last time, it was because he was dreaming of moving to a pig farm in Missouri that he'd read about in *The Budget*.

So that's what this was.

Another one of his daydreams.

Nothing to worry about there. This Levi fellow would probably be gone by the end of the week.

"*Gut* people too," Levi added. "Texans are quite friendly toward Plain folk."

Her *dat* thumped the table. "Sounds *wunderbaar*. Just what I've been thinking of."

Annie didn't answer that. What was the point? This was the way Dat's crazy ideas went. By next week he'd have moved on to raising exotic animals or trying a new crop. She loved her *dat*, loved everything about him, but she'd learned long ago not to worry about his wild ideas. She had a business to run—a thriving wedding-catering business here in Goshen, Indiana. The last thing she needed to concern herself with was pulling up roots and moving to Texas.

Instead, she poured the lemonade into the glasses, smiled at her *dat* and the Amish cowboy sitting at their table and said, "I'll leave you two to your discussion, then. It was nice to meet you, Levi."

"And you."

He tipped the ridiculous hat again and smiled as if she'd said something witty. Not just a cowboy, but a charming one to boot.

Levi spoke with Alton Kauffmann another fifteen minutes. When his wife, Lily, came in and started making dinner, he knew it was time to go.

She smiled at him as she pulled what looked like the mixings of a ham casserole from the refrigerator. "It's nice meeting you, Levi. I hope you'll come visit again."

"Oh, he will," Alton said. "The bishop has come up with a work schedule for Levi, since he's new to the area. He'll be helping me here two afternoons a week—Wednesdays and Fridays."

"We'll expect you to stay for dinner on those days…if you can."

"*Danki.* I appreciate that."

Alton said something about checking on the

horses, so Levi let himself out the front door. Annie was sitting in one of the rockers, writing in a journal. She didn't immediately notice him, and so he was able to study her for a minute.

Young—she couldn't have been over twenty.

Pretty—not that he was interested. He was here to recruit families to move to Texas, not court a woman.

Focused—she still hadn't looked up.

Levi cleared his throat. "Pretty place you have here."

"*Ya*, it is." She finally glanced up. *"Danki."*

"Reminds me a little of Texas, the way the hills stretch out to the west…"

He could still see it in his mind. He wished he had pictures to show her, but of course being Plain they didn't usually fool around with cameras, even the ones on cell phones. He had a few Texas magazines that he'd brought with him. He'd have to remember to bring one over the next afternoon when he came to help Alton.

"You were awfully intent on what you were doing there." He nodded toward her journal.

"Oh. I have a catering business…for Plain weddings. I keep all my notes and calendar in here."

"That's interesting. I've never met an Amish businesswoman before."

"Really? You've never purchased something from a local bakery?"

"Oh, *ya*. Sure."

"Or bought fresh jam?"

"Peach and strawberry." He moved to the rocking chair beside her, placed the knitting basket that was in it on the porch floor and sat.

"All run by women entrepreneurs I would imagine... Plain women entrepreneurs. You can find them in nearly every bakery and fruit stand—not to mention quilt shops and yarn shops. They are also house cleaners and most of our teachers. Schoolhouses aren't a business, but you get my point."

"I do. Obviously, this is a subject you've given a lot of thought."

"I have."

She raised her chin like she had in the kitchen. It almost made him laugh. She was a spunky one.

"I've offended you, and I'm sorry. It wasn't my intention."

She considered him a minute and then closed her journal. "It's possible I'm a little sensitive about the topic, being an entrepreneur myself."

"So tell me about your business."

"Not much to tell. I cater weddings."

"I thought..."

"That the family of the bride cooks the food? *Ya*. A lot of people think that. But when you consider that most of our weddings have over 400 guests...well, the mothers of the bride and groom have an increasingly difficult time cooking for a gathering of that size."

"Maybe they could invite less people."

"And put me out of business? No thank you." Her tone was serious, but she smiled at his joke. "How did you land in Goshen? We're a good ways from Lancaster, Pennsylvania."

Levi didn't respond immediately because the actual answer was complicated. He certainly didn't want to go into his family situation with this young woman he'd known less than twenty minutes. And how could he explain how he'd vowed never to return to this area when he was still just a boy? Goshen did not hold good memories for him, but here he was. He decided to go with the simplest, though less complete answer. "My family knows Simon King. He lived with us in Texas, and he's interested in possibly returning."

"Mamm mentioned you were staying with Simon. We call him Old Simon because there are two others in the congregation—Tall Simon and Young Simon. Young Simon is older than Tall Simon but younger than Old Simon." She laughed and then added, "You know how Plain communities are."

"I do, and he's not that old."

"I'm just surprised he'd be interested in moving at his age."

"I suppose that since his wife died, he's a bit lonely. We stayed in contact over the years. When I mentioned that I was raising up a group to start a new community, he was interested."

"How many families do you need?"

"A dozen is the usual number, with at least one church leader."

"And that would be Old Simon?"

"It would."

"How many families do you have so far?"

"There's myself, Simon and possibly your *dat*."

Annie covered her mouth with her hands. It took Levi a minute to realize she was laughing. It irritated him, though he couldn't have said why.

"What's so funny?"

"I'm sorry." She pulled her lips into a straight line, and stared down at her lap, smoothing out her apron with her fingertips. Obviously, she was making a huge effort to rein in her amusement.

"No, tell me."

"It's only that Dat…"

"Yes?"

"I hope he hasn't raised your hopes. Mamm says he likes to dream, that it's entertainment for him like some people might read a book. It's harmless enough. We've all learned not to take him too seriously in that regard."

Levi stood and pushed his cowboy hat more firmly on his head, but Annie was now on a roll.

"Once he was going to move us to Canada… there are Amish communities there, you know."

"I'm aware."

"Another time, it was a pig farm he was going to purchase, in Missouri, and then there was his idea to raise camels. He checked out a lot of books from the library for that one."

"I would think you'd show more respect for your *dat*. It seems that you don't take what's important to him very seriously."

"You're an expert on my *dat* now?"

"I can tell when a man has a dream."

"Like you?"

"*Ya*, like me."

Annie stood as well and moved a step closer. She gazed up into his face. She looked at him in the same way his mother often had, and it only served to increase his irritation even more. There were always some who were closed-minded, who couldn't see the possibilities of a fresh start in a new place.

"I don't mean to be rude, Levi. However, if you're counting on my family moving to Texas, you should know that's not going to happen."

Instead of contradicting her, he said, "I'm glad I'll have plenty of time to speak to your family about this."

"Speak to them?"

"Since I'll be working here two days a week."

"You're going to be working here?"

"It's nice to meet you, Annie. Perhaps we can continue this conversation tomorrow. Your *mamm* has invited me to stay for dinner."

She crossed her arms and scowled at him as he turned and made his way down the porch steps.

Levi gave her a backward wave, but he didn't look back.

He wanted to. Annie Kauffmann made a pretty picture standing on the front porch with fall leaves pooled at her feet and a cat rubbing against her legs. He didn't allow himself a last glance, though. He knew all about naysayers, people who said it couldn't or shouldn't be done. He'd been stopped by them long enough.

This time, he had a plan.

If things went well, he'd be in Texas by spring.

Chapter Two

Annie managed to avoid Levi on Wednesday when he came to help her father in the fields. They owned a mere eighty acres, but her *dat* used every bit of it. He adamantly believed in varying the crops, which increased the amount of work but also improved the harvest. The hay wouldn't be ready to cut for another two months. The sorghum would need to be harvested by the end of October, soybeans after that, and winter wheat had to be planted as well.

There was always work to be done on a farm.

It wasn't unusual for their bishop to arrange for young Amish men from out of town to find some work, and it was true that her father needed help, but she wasn't sure Levi Lapp was the kind of help he needed. Like the first day he'd spent time with Levi, her *dat* spent Wednesday evening asking enthusiastic questions about Texas over dinner.

"Big ranches there?"

"Some are. The King Ranch is bigger than the state of Rhode Island."

"You don't say."

"Many are smaller family places, though. Like we would have."

Annie and her *mamm* shared a look, but her mother merely shook her head. They'd been through this before. It was best to let the dream run its course. If this went the way of her *dat*'s other ideas, he'd move on to something else before the end of the week. So she endured dinner with Levi and tried to simply nod and appear polite. Had he swallowed an entire encyclopedia of Texas trivia? She couldn't resist commenting when he laughingly told them about the Texas state mammal.

"They have three, actually. The longhorn is the large state mammal. The Mexican free-tailed bat is the flying state mammal. And the nine-banded armadillo is the small state mammal. Those are quite a sight to see. They can run up to thirty miles an hour…"

"Why would they need to run for an hour?"

Levi seemed to consider the question seriously, and Annie was suddenly sorry she'd asked it.

"I suppose they wouldn't. My point is they're

fast, and they can jump straight up too. I've seen them jump…" he held a hand level with the table. "At least that high. It's something else."

Now she was irritated. In truth, she'd been irritated since he'd sat down and started spouting facts and figures. "Aren't they just large rats with shells?"

"More like an anteater or a sloth."

"Who would choose that for their state mammal?"

"Texans would. In fact, they did in 1927." He said all of this slowly, as if she were a child and couldn't grasp the concept.

Her mother jumped in and started talking about the possibility of rain, and Annie soon lost track of the conversation. Thinking back over what she'd said as she washed the dishes, she was rather proud of herself. At least she hadn't laughed at him. She hadn't openly mocked him, but what was his deal? Why did he act as if Texas were the promised land?

She'd simply have to pray for extra strength to curb her tongue when she was around him.

Friday that wasn't so easy.

On Friday, Levi managed to tax her patience to the limit.

It didn't help that she had a wedding the next day, the florist had ordered roses instead of mums and she'd spent ten hours in the kitchen cooking and shredding chicken. When Levi and her father trotted inside, leaving muddy prints across the floor she'd just cleaned, Annie thought she might flip like pancakes on a griddle. Things went downhill from there.

She placed a dish of chicken potpie in the middle of the table. Beside it was a loaf of fresh bread, butter and a large salad. Her *mamm* came in asking about the field work, and they all sat down to eat—including Levi. The serving bowls had barely been passed when her *dat* started in on the Texas trivia points for the day.

"Levi was telling me about Texas longhorns."

Levi held his hands up to his head and then spread them as far apart as possible. "Big longhorns."

"Horns curve outward and can measure up to eight feet in length," her father said. "Sharp on the end, but apparently they're gentle animals."

"Most are." Levi reached for an extra piece of bread. "Best to check with the owner before approaching one."

Annie dropped her fork onto her helping of chicken potpie and gave Levi her most critical look. It always worked when she substituted at their local school, but Levi simply shoveled in another forkful of chicken pie and grinned at her.

"Great dinner," he said after he'd swallowed.

She learned about the rivers that often ran dry,

the terribly hot summer temperatures—her father laughed at that as if such a thing would be eons better than their pleasant summers—and even about their wildflowers.

Finally, she said, "If you'll excuse me, I need to load up my trailer."

"I can help with that," Levi said.

"*Nein*—"

"How kind of you, Levi." Her *mamm* stood and began picking up dishes. "Accept his help, Annie, and your *dat* and I can clean up this kitchen."

Annie couldn't remember the last time she'd seen her father help with the dishes. This was plainly a trick to throw her and Levi together, and she couldn't imagine what her mother was thinking. Unless…maybe she was hoping that she would set Levi straight. She could certainly do that.

"Okay then. *Danki*, Levi. If you'll pick up those boxes of cooked chicken, I'll bring the loaves of bread." The bread tray was clumsier but lighter. The chicken would have taken her at least two trips, but Levi picked up both large boxes and looked around as if he were wondering what else he could carry.

They were barely out the back door when he started in with his questions.

"You have a wedding tomorrow? I thought most Amish weddings were on Tuesday or Thursday."

He was tall and his shadow leaped out in front of them as if it was leading the way. The thought annoyed Annie, though she supposed he had no control over his shadow.

"Tomorrow's wedding is a special situation. This family has relatives who live out of town. They couldn't arrive until late on a Friday afternoon, so we scheduled the wedding for a Saturday."

"You cater a lot of weddings?"

"*Ya*, I do…" She turned toward him when they reached her trailer, ready to confront him about this Texas issue. Then she looked over her shoulder, and the sight of her mobile kitchen eased the knot of tension in her shoulders. "You can bring those inside."

The trailer was small, but she was proud of it. Inside was a mobile kitchen—with dishes for five hundred people, propane-powered refrigerators, three stoves that provided her with a dozen burners, plus a large industrial-sized oven that was six feet tall. On the side, they'd had stenciled the words *Plain & Simple Weddings* in a black italic font.

She set the trays with loaves of fresh bread in the oven. It was taller than she was and would hold the loaves just fine. She didn't have to turn it on, because the loaves were already baked. She'd heat them before the luncheon. When he handed her the boxes of chicken, she took each platter out and set it in one of the propane refrigerators, which she'd turned on earlier in the day.

Levi's eyes widened as he looked around, and he let out a long whistle. "Wow. Some setup you have here."

"It is, and it took time and a lot of work to be able to afford it."

"You pull this with your buggy?"

"No, I don't pull it with my buggy. That would be illegal, not to mention unsafe." She nudged him back out the door of the trailer.

"Then how…"

She waved away his question. She had no intention of telling him the ins and outs of her business. He didn't need to know that she had an *Englisch* partner who owned a large pickup truck. Though she could imagine what Priscilla would say about Levi, and that eased even more of the tension in her neck. Priscilla would call him tall-fair-and-yummy.

She walked out of the trailer and said a quick prayer for patience and wisdom. She seemed to need large helpings of both around Levi Lapp. "I need to talk to you about my *dat*."

"Oh. He's a nice guy. You have a *wunderbaar* family."

"*Ya*, I do." She thought to ask him about his family, but she didn't want to get distracted.

"Look, I wish you well in finding a group to start in Texas…"

"Your *dat* seems quite keen about the idea."

"That's the thing I wanted to talk to you about. Remember what I told you before? Dat gets excited about an idea, usually for about a week."

"Maybe this time is different."

"It isn't."

"How can you know that?"

"Because I know him. He's a *gut* worker, a *gut* provider and a *gut* husband and *dat*. He doesn't smoke or drink or run around."

"Which would make him a great addition to my group."

"We're not moving to Texas!" The words came out more sharply than she'd intended, and for a moment the ever-present smile slipped from Levi's face.

Finally, she was getting through to him.

Or so she thought.

"Change is hard. I understand. And you have this thriving business…"

"Which I have no intention of packing up and moving to Stephenville, Texas."

"Might not be Stephenville. It would depend on where we can find good land at a reasonable price."

"You're missing my point." Maybe she should try appealing to his sense of right and wrong.

"Mamm and I like it here. My *bruders*, they live close enough that they're able to help with the harvest. My *schweschder* lives down the road. We have *freinden* and family here, and I have a thriving business. We. Are. Not. Moving."

She'd moved out in front of him, but he scooted around her and plopped down on the step which led up into the trailer. She stood there, arms crossed, waiting for the truth of what she was saying to sink in beneath his cowboy hat.

"I think what you're actually trying to say is that you'd like me to stop speaking to your *dat* about a move."

"Exactly."

"Would you also like me to quit working for him?"

"What? No. Obviously, he's satisfied with your work, and he needs the help."

"Would you rather I didn't stay for dinner?"

"Of course not. Mamm doesn't mind, and it certainly makes no difference to me."

"So I'm allowed to work here and eat here, but only if I watch what I say."

She was shaking her head before he finished talking. "I'm not the boss of you."

"That's true. You are not."

When he glanced up at her, she was discouraged to see that his normally amiable expression had changed into something more stubborn.

Something probably resembling a Texas mule, if they looked any different than Indiana mules.

She cleared her throat and tried a different approach. "I admire what you're trying to do. I'm simply asking that you consider the situation of my family. We're happy here. Don't stir Dat up with all this talk of longhorns and wildflowers."

"Okay." He stood and clamped the ridiculous cowboy hat down more firmly on his head.

"Okay?"

"Ya."

"Just like that?"

"Seems a fair enough request."

"I agree. That's why I made it."

"Gut day to you then." With a quick smile, he turned and walked toward the lane. As if he'd just thought of something, he stopped, took off the hat, scratched his head and then turned back toward her. "Tell your parents *gut* evening, and *danki* again for the meal."

Annie stared after him, wondering what had just happened.

Why had he agreed so readily?

Why was he smiling?

What was she missing here?

Those things didn't matter. What mattered was that they could put this silly matter of Texas behind them, and she could go back to focusing on her business. Though it was only September, she'd already passed the previous year's profit. Now if she could have a strong fall, she'd feel in a good position for starting the new year.

A new year in Goshen, Indiana, not on the wild plains of Texas.

Amish families tended to eat dinner early— that way they could go out and do the evening chores before things were too dark to see well. The sun had dipped toward the west and a pleasant coolness had settled in as Levi walked down the road, away from the Kauffmans' and toward Old Simon's.

He was thinking of how pretty and stubborn Annie was, how focused she was on that catering business—as if it were all that mattered— and the way her cheeks colored pink when she was angry. He was wondering what it was about himself that irked her so much, when an Amish man working on a fence line called out to him.

"You must be the fellow helping out my father-in-law."

"I'm Levi. Levi Lapp. If your father-in-law is Alton Kauffmann, then *ya*. I'm helping him out two afternoons a week."

"Thought so."

"What gave me away?"

"You're the only Amish person I've ever seen

wearing a cowboy hat. By the way, I'm Jebediah. I'm married to Alton's middle daughter, Nicole."

"Nice to meet you."

Jebediah didn't seem in any hurry to finish mending the fence. Instead he leaned against one of the fence posts and started peppering him with questions. "Heard you're from Texas. What was that like? Also heard you were going back. When do you expect to do that? And do you really think you'll convince Alton to go with you?"

Levi laughed. "It doesn't take long for word to get around."

"You know how it is."

"I do." Levi scanned the horizon and wondered how best to address Jebediah's questions. As usual, his enthusiasm for the subject won out over any instinct that might have told him to approach the subject slowly. "Texas was *wunderbaar*, and I've been trying to get back pretty much since we left, which was twelve years ago when I was fourteen. I hope to move down in the spring. Now that I have a church elder interested—"

"Old Simon?"

"Ya."

"He's not in the best of shape."

"He's not in the worst, either, and once we're there, I think others will come."

"Maybe."

Jebediah's comments were nothing like Annie's. He didn't sound critical of the idea so much as skeptical. A skeptic he could handle.

"You should think about going with us."

"Can't say as I'm interested myself, but if Alton goes, well that might be a different story. My wife is pretty attached to her family, which is *gut* because mine is in Ohio and we can't afford land there."

"Land in Texas is cheap."

"Is it now?" Jebediah grinned as if he'd heard that one before. "Cheap doesn't really matter if you don't have any money, which I don't. Married four years ago, and we have three *boppli* with another on the way. Every cent I makes gets plucked from my hand like a north wind snatched it away."

"That doesn't bother you?"

"Not really. We have what we need."

Levi wasn't sure how to answer that. It was a common sentiment among Amish men and women alike. He had a little trouble relating. It wasn't that he wanted more. It was only that he wanted something different than what he had.

"I don't want to keep you from mending that fence, and I best get on before Old Simon wonders what happened to me."

"See you tomorrow then."

"Tomorrow?" Levi had already turned away, but now he turned back to Jebediah. "Oh, I don't work for Alton on Saturdays. That's my day to stay and help Old Simon."

He'd even started calling the old guy that, and he'd only learned the nickname recently.

"I mean that I'll see you at the wedding."

"Wedding?"

"Beth and Avery. Old Simon will be there for sure and certain—everyone will. It'll be a *gut* time for you to meet folks."

The wedding that Annie had been preparing for. He suddenly realized that he'd like to see her in action, serving the masses from her tiny trailer. "I don't even know them."

"You're invited nonetheless. You're a part of our community now. Everyone's invited."

Those words echoed through Levi's mind as he walked the last half mile to Old Simon's house. *You're a part of our community now.* It was a simple yet common sentiment among Plain folks. You moved in; you were accepted.

So why had he never felt at home in Lancaster?

Why did he have such terrible memories of his time here in Goshen?

Maybe because he'd resented his community's decision from the day they'd abandoned the Texas community. Maybe because the move had been difficult for his parents, not to mention his siblings. The old ache twisted in his gut, but he chose to ignore it.

That was his past.

His future was to the south and moving closer every day.

He arrived home to find Simon sitting on the back porch, an open Bible in his lap. He barely seemed to look down at the well-worn pages. In fact, Levi had surmised that the old guy's eyesight had weakened to the point that he couldn't read the words printed there, but it seemed to soothe him to hold the open Bible.

He also was a terrible driver. It was a good thing that the buggy horse practically drove itself, or they would have been killed on Levi's first day in town.

"Preparing for your sermon?"

"Ya." Simon looked up in surprise, so apparently, he hadn't heard Levi enter through the front door or the banging of the back screen door as he'd come outside. Maybe his hearing was going too, but a smile spread across his face.

He was a nice old guy, terribly lonely since his wife had died the year before. Their children were in Kentucky. Levi had written to both sons before he had accepted Old Simon's invitation to move to Goshen. He didn't want to be the source of hard feelings in the family. The eldest son had explained that they were trying to convince Simon to move, but that so far he'd resisted. Levi didn't share with Jonah his hopes that Simon would move to Texas with him. He didn't lie about it. The subject just didn't come up.

Old Simon patted the Bible. "*Gotte*'s word— it's a lamp for my feet and a light for my path."

"Is that what your sermon will be on?" Levi eased onto the floor of the porch, bracing his back against the porch column.

"Maybe," Simon said. "As the Lord leads."

"I met Jebediah this afternoon."

"He's a *gut* man and about your age, if I remember right."

"Told me about the wedding tomorrow."

Simon's expression turned to one of concern, but then he tapped his forefinger against the arm of the rocker and said, "I knew there was something I was forgetting. We have a wedding tomorrow."

"He said I was welcome to attend, even though I don't know Beth and Avery."

"Who?"

"The couple getting married."

"Oh. That's right. It is a *gut* idea for you to go. I assumed you would. Weddings are a *gut* place to meet people, and maybe a young lady will catch your eye." Simon grinned and then turned his attention out to the family garden. He hadn't put that in himself. A neighbor must have done it for him. He didn't seem to see the last of the vegetables that waited to be gathered, though. Instead he spoke of the past. "Did I ever tell you where I met my *fraa*, Tabitha?"

"You didn't."

"It was at a local wedding. I knew the minute I saw her that she was the one." He pressed his fingertips against his chest. "Something in my heart…just told me."

Levi didn't know how to answer that, so he stood and said, "I ate with the Kauffmanns. Have you had anything yet?"

Simon shook his head and turned his eyes back to the pages of his Bible. "Can't say as I'm hungry."

"I'll go and fix you an egg with some of that ham we had left over. You need to eat."

"*Ya.* Okay."

Levi walked into the kitchen and set about putting together a simple meal for the old man. Working in the kitchen reminded him of Annie's lecture about women entrepreneurs. Levi was fine with that. He didn't see any problem with women starting businesses. In his experience, they often had excellent perspectives on what customers wanted to purchase.

He actually admired her for starting an Amish catering business, but he sensed that her passion might become a roadblock for his own plans. Alton wouldn't want to leave unless his entire family was behind the idea. And Annie obviously was dead set against it. It wasn't absolutely necessary to have Alton in his group, but it would help. And it might mean that Jebediah and his family would come, as well.

All he had to do was win Annie over to the idea.

Which, he knew, would be no simple task.

As he heated the cast-iron pan, fried an egg and put it on the plate with fresh bread and a slice of ham, he thought of the words of his *daddi*.

No dream comes true unless you wake up and go to work.

He'd known it wouldn't be easy to start a community in Texas, but he was willing to work. He only had to convince ten more families and then they could send two men down to look for land. Goshen was a big community. Regardless what Annie said, he thought that Alton would follow through on this dream. Indiana Amish weren't as set in their ways like Pennsylvania Amish, or at least that was how it seemed so far.

Then again, he could be merely seeing what he wanted to see. Time would tell—though he didn't have much of that. They needed to form a group, decide on some basic rules and then send down scouts. They needed to do all of those things in the next few months. After all, planting season in Texas started early.

Chapter Three

Levi didn't have a chance to talk to many people before the wedding. Amish weddings started rather early in the day—on account of they were long and they needed to be finished in time for lunch. Then there were games for the young adults and children, and after that, most of the teens and young married folk stayed for dinner.

Beth and Avery's ceremony was taking place outside, so it was fortunate that the day dawned mild and sunny. In fact, it was a perfect fall day. He watched families assemble across the benches that had been set out in the backyard of the Stutzman farm, but his mind was on Annie Kauffmann. He'd had only one glimpse of her when he and Old Simon were walking from their buggy to the house. He was thinking of how he hoped to have time to talk to Alton again when he spied Annie darting from her trailer toward the back porch.

How did she manage to move that trailer there?

When did she find the time to cook enough food for all of these people?

Did she enjoy cooking that much?

And why wasn't she married? She was a nice-enough-looking woman and pleasant, other than her dislike of Texas. Or maybe it was him that she disliked. It was hard to tell.

He was chasing that line of thought when the hymn singing started. Old Simon led the congregation in a prayer, then there was more singing, a short sermon, and finally, the soon-to-be-married couple stood in front of everyone.

It seemed to him like they'd only been there a few minutes. He was surprised when he glanced at his watch and saw that ninety minutes had already passed.

As he watched the couple exchange their vows, his mind slipped back to Annie. Did she need help readying the wedding lunch? Probably not. No doubt she'd catered many weddings before without his help, but then again, perhaps volunteering would soften her up a little.

Before he could properly think that through, they were singing again and then the bishop—an older guy named Marcus with a beard that was more salt than pepper—reminded everyone to stay for the meal and led them in a time of silent blessing. The next thing Levi knew, Jebediah appeared at his side holding two babies in his arms and introduced him to at least a dozen people. It would take him a while to get all the names straight, but he tried to look as if he were paying attention. The names were common Amish names—Joel, Matthew, Silas, Eli, Martha, Tabitha, Naomi. He wondered how he would ever remember who was who, but then he realized he wasn't staying in Goshen. It didn't really matter if he remembered everyone's name. So he smiled politely and said hello.

Finally, a woman and a young girl moved beside Jebediah. The woman said something softly to him, as the young girl clung to her dress. Jebediah laughed and turned to Levi.

"This is my wife, Nicole."

"Oh, *ya*? *Gut* to meet you."

"Jebediah told me all about you."

He could see the family resemblance, now that he studied her closely. She had the same warm eyes as Annie, but her hair was blonder and she had her father's height. Annie was shorter with hair that reminded him of the color of autumn wheat. The word *prettier* popped into his mind, but he brushed it away. Annie Kauffmann might be pretty, but she had a lot of strong opinions that she didn't mind sharing. It might be funny except for the fact that she was standing in the way of his plans.

"I think we lost him for a minute," Nicole said.

"He drifts off every now and then." Jebediah jostled the two babies in his arms.

"I can hear you. I was thinking of how much you look like your sister Annie."

"*You* look exactly like Annie described. She's talked about you a fair amount." Nicole reached out and wiped some drool off one of the babes in Jebediah's arms. "As has Dat."

"All *gut* things I hope."

"From Dat? *Ya.* But Annie, well…you know how Annie is."

"I do? I've only known her a few days."

"She's not exactly a mystery."

"Meaning?"

"She told me she told you that she doesn't like all this Texas talk."

"I guess she did mention it."

Jebediah and Nicole both laughed at that as if he'd told a joke. It made him squirm, not that they might be laughing at him, but that he might be up against a force to be reckoned with. Instead of delving into the details of Annie's opposition, he changed the subject.

"What are your children's names?"

"The twins are Micah and Mitchell—nine

months old." Jebediah readjusted both babies in his arms. "Our oldest is Rachel."

"I'm three," Rachel proclaimed, holding up a pudgy hand and bending down her thumb and pinky.

Levi remembered what Jebediah had said about their expecting another. He glanced at Nicole's stomach, then quickly averted his eyes.

She again laughed. "I'm five months along, in case you were wondering."

"I wasn't." And now his cheeks were burning.

When everyone else surged forward to be in the first seating of folks who would eat, Levi hung back.

"You can come with us into the first group," Jebediah said.

"No need. I don't mind waiting. Gives me time to watch folks."

Annie had stepped out of the trailer to deliver two platters of food. When she stepped back inside a small tabby cat crept in after her.

"Uh-oh," Jebediah said.

His astute comment was immediately followed by an ear-piercing scream. He handed the babies off to Nicole, but Levi was already on his way toward Annie.

The scene in front of him when he stepped into the trailer was something he wouldn't forget for a very long time.

An *Englisch* woman was holding two large bowls of side dishes up high and trying to move around Annie without dropping them. She wore a conservative dress and a handkerchief over her hair, which was red and braided into a long ponytail down her back. She most certainly was not Amish.

Annie wore a light gray Amish dress with a white apron. A fresh *kapp* covered her hair, and her cheeks were a bright red. She had a pot lid in one hand and a dish towel in the other. She was slapping at the cat with the towel and holding the pot lid like an early Christian in Rome's Colosseum fending off the hungry lions.

As for the cat, he was clearly a terrified kitten, but that didn't stop him from arching his back and hissing at Annie.

Levi wanted to see how this would unfold. He wanted to burst out laughing, but another look at Annie told him that wouldn't be a wise move.

So instead, he pulled off his Stetson, dropped it over the unsuspecting cat, scooped it up in his arms and fled the trailer.

"Who was that?" Priscilla was still holding the two dishes of corn casserole high, as if the cat might return at any moment and leap on the food.

"I'll explain later. We need to get this food out there."

The next hour passed in a blur of activity. Annie loved nearly every minute of it. She liked feeding people, liked seeing the bride and groom and families relax. This was their day of celebration. They shouldn't be worried about chicken and hot rolls and casserole dishes. The fact that she did her job well meant that they could enjoy the wedding. And she didn't mind admitting that she was very good at guiding families through these special days, when there weren't feral cats hopping into her trailer.

She sighed and stood in the doorway looking out over the tables.

"Take a break," Priscilla said. "In fact, take some food and go sit down somewhere."

"You're bossy, you know that?"

"Which is why I make a good partner."

"I guess."

"You're still staring at him."

"Who?"

"The Amish cowboy."

Annie snorted at that. It sounded so ridiculous. It was ridiculous.

"So what gives?"

"He arrived here a few days ago."

"Why?"

"Looking for families to move to Texas."

"I didn't realize there were Amish communities there."

"There's one, and it's quite small and located in South Texas. Levi wants to start another."

"Ahhhh…" Priscilla's single word said she finally understood the problem. She'd been around Annie long enough to know how excited her *dat* could be when he first dove into a new idea.

"We're not moving," Annie said.

"Have you told your *dat* that?"

"You can't tell Dat anything. You have to… wait it out."

"Like the camels."

"*Ya*. Like that."

"If it's any consolation, I have family in Texas—Fort Worth. I've visited a few times. It's not such a bad place to live."

Annie shook her head and picked at the plate of food that Priscilla had pushed into her hand. "I need a plan."

"Uh-oh."

"What if Dat went through with it? I mean usually he doesn't, but this time could be different. I've never seen him this focused before. He even checked out some books on Texas from the library. Spent some time on their computers looking things up too."

"That does sound serious."

"I need a plan to distract Levi."

"What did you have in mind?"

"I don't know. What are men interested in…"

At that moment, a swell of laughter arose from the newlyweds' table. Both Annie and Priscilla stuck their heads out of the trailer to see the bride blushing and the groom ducking his head.

"Women," they said at the same time.

"That's it." Annie reached for her glass of tea and made her way down the trailer steps.

"Do you need help?" Priscilla called after her.

Annie turned so that she was walking backward. "You already helped. You gave me the idea."

"I did?"

She made her way to an empty seat, sat down and enjoyed the plate of food. The chicken had not dried out, the vegetable casseroles were tasty and the bread practically melted in her mouth. She was a good cook, a good businesswoman, and she wasn't going to lose everything she'd built to a guy who had stumbled into town with a dream.

It was later that afternoon before she had a chance to implement her plan. She and Priscilla had cleaned the dishes and made sure everything was ready for the evening meal. With nearly two hours before they had to do anything else, Priscilla decided to drive into town and do some shopping. Annie made her way to the pasture fence, where Beth's parents kept their small herd of goats. They were playful animals. One stuck its nose through the fence when she approached, so she reached into her pocket and pulled out a piece of carrot.

"Now they're going to stampede over here." Levi walked up and crossed his arms on the top of the fence.

"Maybe that's what I wanted."

"A goat stampede?"

She dusted off her hands and shooed the goat away. "I saw you talking to Dat earlier."

Levi raised his hands in surrender. "Not the way you think."

"So you weren't talking to him about Texas?"

"I didn't bring it up. I told you I wouldn't, and I didn't."

"But…"

"I didn't say I wouldn't answer questions. He brought it up because he had a few questions that cropped up from his reading."

"And it didn't hurt that a few other men were standing around listening."

Now Levi smiled. "Come on, Annie. It's why I'm here. You can't fault me for that."

"Except your plan could bankrupt my business."

"Ten families moving wouldn't affect you at all."

She shook her head so hard that her *kapp* strings bounced back and forth. She had promised herself she wouldn't get into an argument with him. That wasn't her plan.

But she needed for him to see what was at stake.

Suddenly she thought of the brainstorming sessions she'd had with Priscilla, before they'd started Plain & Simple Weddings. Part of their initial challenge had been convincing families that they needed their services, and that in the end, it would be less expensive for them. She was up against the same sort of thing with Levi. He simply didn't understand that he needed her services, and she wasn't talking about catering.

Levi Lapp thought he needed a fresh start, but that wasn't the case at all. When had moving away from your problems ever solved anything?

Levi didn't need to move; he needed to believe in himself.

He needed to be able to envision his future here—in Goshen, Indiana.

He needed a woman, and she knew several that were available.

Annie cleared her throat and looked back toward her trailer. "Priscilla and I started our business three years ago."

He seemed surprised at the change of subject, but he turned as she had and looked out at the trailer.

"She put up two-thirds of the initial money."

"You mean buying the trailer?"

"It's actually a mobile kitchen and cost a little more than twelve thousand dollars."

Levi glanced at her in surprise. "Seriously?"

"*Ya*. Stoves, refrigerators and enough dishes for five hundred...not to mention the trailer itself and the licensing fees."

"I had no idea."

"We broke even the first year."

"Wow."

"She's a *gut* partner too. Since she's *Englisch*, she drives a truck that can pull the trailer. She can also order a lot of what we need wholesale on the computer."

"You're saying you two make a *wunderbaar* team. I can see that. You have every right to be proud of what you've done, Annie."

"Pride goes before destruction as my *mamm* often reminds me, but I am pleased with our success. More importantly I enjoy what we do. I like making this..." She waved at the large group of people sprawled across the green yard—full, content, some of them growing sleepy. "I like making it all possible. I enjoy seeing others happily wed."

"What about you?"

"Me?" Her thoughts scrambled for an answer to his question. It wasn't the first time someone had asked her why she wasn't married, but somehow it was different coming from Levi Lapp while he smiled at her with his cowboy hat tilted at an angle.

"Doesn't being at so many weddings make you…interested in finding someone?"

"I'm only twenty-four."

"I didn't say you were an old maid."

"My *mamm* worries about that, but I'm in no hurry. I've been to my *schweschder*'s often enough to know that running a catering business is less work than three small children." She paused, and then added, "What about you?"

"Me?" His voice squeaked. He cleared his throat and resettled his hat on his head. "I figure that will happen after I move to Texas."

"But what if you could find a *fraa* here and take her with you?"

"Now you're making fun of me."

"I'm not."

"Did you have someone in mind?" The grin he gave her reminded Annie of the cat in her trailer—mischievous and daring.

Annie had a flash of clarity then, staring up into Levi's blue eyes. There was no doubt that she could find women in their congregation interested in dating Levi Lapp, but she wouldn't be able to trick him into it. That part of her plan died before she could implement it. Levi was like competition that you had to face head-on.

So she stepped back and crossed her arms. "Do

you really think you can convince my *dat* and *bruder* to move to Texas?"

"I'm not saying that I can, but it should be their decision…along with your *mamm* and your *schweschder*. If it's what they want, then you should be happy for them."

She didn't bother arguing that her *mamm* and *schweschder* were quite happy in Goshen. Levi was like a steam-engine train headed in one direction—no U-turns allowed.

"All right. I'll make you a deal."

"A deal?"

"You agree to date some of my *freinden*…"

"Date?"

"Hear me out. You're not planning on staying. They're not necessarily looking to get married, but they need…let's say they need a little experience in the dating area."

Levi groaned. "You're going to set me up with the rejects."

She felt a headache forming just at her left temple. Closing her eyes, she prayed to *Gotte* for patience, then counted to three.

"They're shy," she corrected him. "And maybe they have a lack of confidence. Dating you should help that."

"Because I'm such a *gut* catch?"

He grinned, and she realized he was handsome.

Not her type, but handsome nonetheless. Yes, this plan could work.

"Let's say there's no pressure on either side. That should help. They'll know you're not staying..."

"And I'll know they're not really interested. This is a terrible plan. Why would I agree to it?"

This was the tricky part. She almost couldn't believe she was going to suggest it. But then again, what choice did she have? He was going to talk to her *dat* and Jebediah in spite of how much it bothered her. They would keep asking him questions. He'd keep painting pictures of rosy Texas sunsets.

"When were you planning to leave?"

"You get right to the point, don't you?"

"Do you even have a plan?"

"Of course I do." Levi scuffed the toe of his boot against the dirt, and she noticed he was wearing Western boots. Of course he was.

"Why does our bishop let you dress like that?"

"This?" He pointed the toe of his boot up. "These are Ariats. Very comfortable."

"And that." She pointed at his hat.

"A Stetson. All Texans wear them."

"Why are *you* wearing them? You're Amish." She said the last word slowly, in two drawn-out syllables.

"Marcus talked to me about it," Levi admitted.

"He said if I decided to join the community I'd need to dress more conservatively. I assured him I was moving on, so he said it wasn't a problem."

"Back to the *when* of your plan…"

"I hope to go down before Christmas to look for land and move by early spring—my target date is February or March."

"That's not spring."

"It is in Texas."

She couldn't hold the sigh inside. She'd hoped he was planning for a move in a year, which would have been plenty of time for her *dat*'s attention to wander elsewhere. A scouting party before Christmas? That was mere months away. She'd have to work fast if she hoped to save the nice comfortable life she had. She'd already waded in too far to back out now, plus she didn't have any backup plan. It wasn't going to be easy to match Levi with someone. Who wanted an Amish cowboy? Though there was one possibility…

Levi was studying her as if expecting her to give up. He didn't know her very well. She liked a challenge. She thrived in tough situations. Tossing her *kapp* strings behind her shoulders, she plastered on what she hoped was her prettiest smile. "All right. You agree to date a couple of my friends…not at the same time, mind you."

"Of course not."

"And in return, I won't try and stop you from talking to my family about your plans."

"As if you could."

"My point is that you won't have to deal with my objections."

He studied her a minute and then said, "Seriously?"

"Ya."

"What's in it for you?"

"Me?"

"Why are you doing this? I know you're dead set against the idea of moving."

"Oh, I am not moving. I'll find a way to stay here even if you convince the whole community to move south."

Levi laughed. "That's the Annie I know."

"You don't know me."

"Uh-huh. But seriously, why are you doing this?"

"I like weddings is all. I enjoy seeing two people who are meant to be together find each other."

"I'm not getting married."

"I know, but maybe *Gotte* has different plans."

"What does *Gotte* have to do with it?"

"Maybe He brought you to Goshen for a reason…a different reason."

"So now you're a matchmaker?"

"Think of me as a concerned bystander."

Levi shook his head. "I don't know…"

"Is it a deal or not? If you'd rather, I can keep pointing out all the terrible things about your Lone Star State."

"All right. It's a deal." He held out his hand. "But you have to shake on it."

She rolled her eyes, but put her hand in his. He closed his fingers around hers, held her hand long enough that she didn't like the goose bumps running down her arm or the jumble of nerves in her stomach. She jerked her hand away.

"Great. Then it's settled. I'll give you the name of your first date when you come over on Wednesday to work."

"I look forward to it."

Of course he did. The man was conceited in addition to being stubborn. But, just possibly, she'd found a way to keep her life firmly rooted in Goshen, because she had the perfect woman in mind for Levi Lapp and this person would never consider moving away. All Annie had to do was see to it that the two of them fell in love. She was envisioning a wedding announcement before the holidays if she handled this right. No need for a long courtship at their age. It would mean she'd have to live around Levi the rest of her life, but at least she wouldn't have to do so in Texas.

Chapter Four

Annie woke the next morning determined to start right away on her new plan. Levi Lapp had invaded her dreams throughout the night—she'd found herself surrounded by wildflowers, nose to nose with a longhorn, even looking across a vast plain toward rain clouds in the distance. As if those images of Texas weren't bad enough, Levi himself had put in several appearances, always wearing his Stetson hat and that cocky grin.

It was past time to do something proactive and push Levi and his Texas trivia out of her dreams. She picked her newest Sunday dress, brushed her hair vigorously and wove it into a braid tight enough to pucker the skin along her forehead. Pulling the covers up snug on her bed, she prayed for wisdom and patience. She was bound to need both.

Her *mamm* found her downstairs making coffee before the sun was up.

"Problem sleeping, dear?" Her *mamm* stared at the coffee maker on the stove as if she could make it percolate faster.

"Go sit down. I'll bring it to you."

"All right."

Five minutes later, they were both clutching steaming mugs of coffee and sitting at the kitchen table.

"Want to talk about it?" Her *mamm* kept blinking her eyes, as if she wasn't quite awake yet.

"About what?"

"Whatever's bothering you."

"Nothing's bothering me."

Instead of arguing, her mother took another sip of the dark brew—the entire Kauffmann family enjoyed their coffee strong—and waited.

"Oh, all right. I'll admit it. This thing with Levi has worked its way under my *kapp*."

"Has it now?"

"I don't want to move to Texas, Mamm."

"Which is understandable."

"It is?"

"I want to be where your father is, and if he decides—"

Annie groaned. "Tell me you're not on their side."

"This isn't about us and them. This is about

seeking out and following *Gotte's wille* for our lives. I'm not afraid of doing that even if it means living in a different place."

"I'm not afraid. It's just that if Levi had never shown up on our doorstep, Dat would never be considering a move to Texas."

"Perhaps, but *Gotte* brings people into our lives for a reason."

Annie jumped up to refill their mugs. As she turned toward the stove, she muttered, "I'm pretty sure it was a Greyhound bus that brought Levi to us."

"And yet *Gotte* put this dream in Levi's heart."

"Oops. I didn't mean for you to hear that."

"Levi's relationship with Old Simon also brought him here."

Annie refilled her *mamm*'s mug and then plopped down in the chair across from her. She needed her mother with her on this. Perhaps she should try a different tack.

"Okay. Let's assume what you're saying is true…"

Her *mamm*'s eyebrows arched, but she didn't interrupt.

"But what if Levi is confusing some unre- solved business from his childhood as *Gotte*'s leading? Maybe *Gotte* brought him here for a reason—a reason other than ripping twelve of our families away to start a new community. Maybe Goshen needs Levi here, but he doesn't realize it yet." For some reason, that idea didn't sit well with her, either. In her daydreams, Levi had always ridden off toward the West, tilting his hat against the setting sun, searching for another community where he could disrupt people's lives.

"What I mean is that perhaps *Gotte* has other plans for him. We can't know."

"Indeed."

They were silent for a moment. Finally her *mamm* said, "Do you have some ideas about why Levi might be here?"

Annie picked at a fingernail. "Maybe he's supposed to meet someone here."

"Someone?"

"A woman, Mamm. Maybe he's supposed to meet a woman, fall in *lieb*, settle down and start a family." Once she said it out loud, the plan took on a new dimension. What she was suggesting was possible. It was almost as if she were doing a charitable thing for him. "I spoke with Levi yesterday after the wedding, and he's agreed to allow me to set him up on a few dates."

"That's kind of you."

"I guess, but just think, Mamm…if he falls in *lieb*, then he might forget this ridiculous obsession with Texas."

"Mmm-hmm."

"He might decide he wants to stay here in Goshen."

"I suppose that's possible."

"And if he stays, well, we both know that Dat's enthusiasm for moving will melt away."

Instead of arguing with her, which was what Annie had suspected, her *mamm* smiled over the rim of her mug. "Who did you have in mind to set him up with?"

"Martha Weaver."

"Have you spoken to Martha about this?"

"*Nein.* I was hoping to do so after church service."

Her *mamm* drained her coffee cup, stood and pushed her chair back in under the table. Walking around behind Annie, she kissed her on top of the head, causing Annie to feel four years old again.

She thought that her mother would reprimand her, tell her to mind her own business, caution her about intervening in other people's lives. She didn't. Instead, she simply walked to the refrigerator, pulled out what she planned to cook for breakfast and began cracking eggs into a bowl—leaving Annie to wonder what she wasn't saying. If she were honest with herself, some doubts remained in her mind about this new plan. Perhaps she was foolish to think that playing matchmaker could solve her problem.

* * *

It was well after lunch before Annie had a chance to speak with Martha. She'd been friends with Martha since their school days. Though Martha was two years younger, she'd always seemed to be around Annie's age, perhaps because she'd stepped into the role of helping with her younger siblings. Annie found her watching over her disabled brother as well as a group of the younger children who were playing in a pile of leaves in the circle of three giant maple trees. The service had been held at the Bontragers' place. The old couple had raised a family of twelve in Goshen. All their children—all twelve of them— had moved to Maine, and the small For Sale sign in the front yard reminded Annie that they would be joining them soon. The Bontragers had been around as long as Annie could remember.

Why would they move?

Why did things have to change?

Plainly they were happy here.

She shook away the questions and reminded herself to focus on her mission.

Walking over to Martha, she held out her arms to accept one of the Miller babies that her friend was holding. "Joseph or Jeremiah?"

The twins were six months old, but she still couldn't tell the difference between them.

"Joseph. You can tell because he has a little strawberry mark on the back of his neck."

Annie snuggled the baby against her neck and sat down at the picnic table that had been positioned under the trees. "Where's the older *bruder*?"

"Stephen has a little cold, so Kathy took him inside to see if he'd nap. I was already watching over the others, so two more didn't seem like a problem."

There were six children of various ages running around, some falling in the leaves, some sitting on the ground and crushing the brittle red, yellow and orange leaves in their fists. Off to the side sat Martha's brother.

Annie had known Thomas all of her life. She didn't see him as disabled so much as she saw her best friend's twin brother. Sometimes, though, when they were in town shopping or splurging on ice cream, she'd notice the way strangers looked at Thomas. In those moments she'd have a tiny inkling of what it was like for Martha and why she was so fiercely protective of him.

Tommy, or Big Tom as he liked to be called, had a flat nose and small ears. He had been diagnosed with Down syndrome the day after his birth. At twenty-two, his body had grown to that of a man, but he still acted like a child in many ways.

Amish families have the highest incidence of twins of any demographic group—a teacher had mentioned that in class one day and Annie had looked around the room to spot no less than six pairs of twins. Annie understood that the bond between twins was strong, but the bond between Martha and Thomas exceeded even that. It was as if they were tethered together by some invisible line—a spiritual cord stronger than any rope made by man.

Martha seemed content to watch the children and her brother. She was mature for her age and bore an air of complete contentment. She wore glasses—blue frames she'd found on sale at the local optometrist office—had beautiful white-blond hair and blue eyes.

Those eyes were now studying her, brows slightly arched, a smile playing on her lips.

Annie jumped up, still snuggling baby Joseph and pacing back and forth in front of Martha. Another glance at her friend confirmed that she'd have a higher chance of success if she got straight to the point.

"Levi Lapp would like to step out with you."

Martha's mouth fell open, and she looked over her shoulder as if Annie might be talking to someone else.

"How do you know Levi?" Martha asked. "He just moved here…"

Annie blushed. "He was at our house last week, talking to my *dat* about Texas."

A toddler ran over to Martha and held up his arms. She shifted Jeremiah to her left arm and pulled the toddler into her lap. "Why would Levi Lapp want to step out with me?"

"Why wouldn't he? You're a pleasant person, Martha, and very eligible. Let's not forget that."

"I rarely do."

"You're pretty, and you have a good head on your shoulders."

"He couldn't possibly know what kind of head I have on my shoulders. So stop trying to butter me up and just tell me what's really going on."

Annie groaned. She should have known Martha wouldn't make this easy.

"He wants to move to Texas."

"Why do you care about that?"

"He wants to start a community there, and he's targeting our community to pull families from."

"Targeting?"

"Whatever." She waved away Martha's concern about her word choice. "He's been bending my *dat*'s ear, and now Dat is stirred up."

"Ahh. Now your concern makes sense. But what does this have to do with me?"

"I need to distract him."

"That's what you want me to do?"

"*Nein. Ya.* Maybe." Baby Joseph had fallen

asleep in her arms, so Annie sat on the ground in front of the picnic table, crossed her legs and placed him in the crook of her knee. She quickly explained that Levi was working at their house two days a week and that he had set his sights on recruiting her father and brother.

"Jebediah and Nicole might move to Texas?"

"I don't know. Anything is possible, I guess."

"Wow."

"I know."

"Texas?"

"You should hear him talk about it. Actually, you *will* hear him talk about it if you go out on a date with him because it's his only topic of conversation."

"Hmm. You make him sound more attractive all the time."

Annie snorted. "He's good-looking enough, I'll give you that, but that's not the point. I just want you to agree to go out with him a few times."

"Again…why? You know I'm taking a six-month break from dating."

"Ya."

"After what happened with David—"

"It wasn't your fault he left the faith. He would have been willing to move to Alaska if they'd let him keep that cell phone."

They shared a smile, both remembering the way that David had carried it around, glancing at it every few minutes, tapping on it constantly with his fingers.

"That relationship was never going to work anyway," Martha admitted. "But the fact remains that I'm on a roll of bad relationships."

"Only three."

"Four if you count Meno."

"Years ago, and he was never right for you."

"None of them are." Instead of looking as if that thought depressed her, Martha smiled. "I'm on a break."

"Okay. All right. So don't call it a date. Call it being a friend to someone new in our community."

"It doesn't have to be romantic?"

"*Nein.* Levi thinks…"

"Uh-oh. What did you tell him?"

"I might have mentioned that you need practice dating."

"We both know that isn't the case."

"You need practice dating someone new."

"Let me get this straight. I'm supposed to go out with him and distract him…"

"Maybe mention the *gut* points about Goshen. You know this place as well as I do, and it's a fine community. He doesn't have to go to Texas to find a place to settle down."

"I'm not falling in love with Levi Lapp."

"Of course not."

"I don't want to move to Texas any more than you do."

"Exactly."

"He's bound to figure that out sooner than later."

"Later would be better. Just buy me some time for Dat to simmer down about the idea."

"Why don't you do it? Why don't you date him?"

Annie shook her head so hard that her *kapp* strings bounced back and forth. "Oh no. That would only encourage him to get closer to my family. Plus, fall and spring are the busiest seasons for my business. I have no time to waste on dating."

"Oh, but I should…"

"You know what I mean. It's fine for other people. I want other people to date."

"If they didn't, you'd be out of business."

"Exactly."

Martha placed the toddler on the ground and baby Jeremiah in his baby carrier. She stood, stretched and cast a look toward Big Tom who was still playing in the leaves, though now he was lying on his back and making a snow angel—or maybe a leaf angel. Martha smiled, and Annie was struck again by how close the two were.

Annie handed Joseph back to Martha, stood and brushed off the back of her dress.

"Will you do it?"

"*Ya, ya,* I'll do it."

"*Danki.*"

"But only because you're my best friend."

"I owe you."

"*Ya.* You do." Martha walked over to her *bruder*, who held up a hand and allowed her to pull him to his feet.

Annie glanced up in time to see Levi driving away in Old Simon's buggy. She'd missed talking to him today, but that was okay. She'd tell him the good news first thing Wednesday.

By the time Levi showed up at the Kauffmann place on Wednesday, he'd completely forgotten Annie's plan to find him a girl. He'd been focused on other things. He'd talked with several of the local families at the wedding, and three had come back to ask him questions after the church service. At this rate, he might get to Texas earlier than he'd thought. He might have enough interest to send down a scouting group before fall turned into winter.

He was mucking out the horse stalls early Wednesday morning, before they'd even had breakfast, when Annie showed up in the barn.

"*Gude mariye,* Levi."

He wiped the sweat out of his eyes and squinted at her.

As usual, she looked fresh and energetic. Normally she seemed aggravated when she saw him, as if she'd swallowed unsweetened lemonade. Today she was smiling broadly. Why the change in attitude?

Then he remembered their deal and literally slapped himself on the forehead.

"Problem?"

"Just remembering what you talked me into."

"I didn't talk you into anything. I simply made a suggestion and you agreed."

She grinned at him as she had on Saturday. He could still feel her hand in his, the way her eyes had widened as she'd glanced up into his eyes, and then how she'd snatched her hand away as if she'd been stung by a bee. What was that about?

She didn't waste any time ruining his morning. She pulled a folded sheet of paper from her apron pocket and waved it at him. "I wrote down the information you need for your date."

"My date…"

Her plan was bound to be a trap. He didn't know how, but he was sure that it must be designed to ruin his goal of moving to Texas.

"Her name is Martha Weaver. Here are directions to her house as well as the number for the nearest phone shack."

He took the piece of paper and stared down at her tidy handwriting. "Guess I'm stuck doing this."

"You're lucky to date Martha, actually. She's levelheaded, nice looking—"

"Then why isn't she courting or married? There must be something wrong with her."

"And she's my best friend."

"Oops. Sorry if what I said sounded rude."

"It did, but I'm not surprised. Men your age only want to step out with the prettiest, thinnest girls."

"That's not true."

Instead of arguing, Annie walked into the stall and around the perimeter. "Martha has a sweet tooth. You might think about taking her to the pie pantry."

"I have dated before, you know."

"Oh, you have?"

"Don't look so surprised."

"I'm not surprised."

He could tell that she was holding in her laughter, which irritated him more than it probably should have.

"I wonder if your *mamm* has breakfast ready."

"Oh, *ya*. That's what I came out to tell you."

"You could have led with that."

"And miss the chance to tease you?"

"Is that what you're doing? And why are you in such a chipper mood this morning?"

"Who wouldn't be in a good mood on such a beautiful morning?"

He had been too—until Annie showed up with her dating instructions. He hadn't fully thought this through when he'd agreed to her dating scheme. His few attempts to date back in Lancaster had been a disaster. The women he'd met were only interested in settling down and having babies. He had nothing against either, but they'd had no patience for his talk of moving to Texas, especially when they'd heard that he was saving every dime in order to make the move possible.

Dreamer.

Naive.

Immature.

He'd been called all sorts of things, always with a smile, a touch on the shoulder, and a look of pity. Well, he didn't need anyone's approval or sympathy, and he didn't need another woman who was going to try and set him straight.

"What are you frowning about?"

Instead of answering, he carried the pitchfork into the main room of the barn, then returned to pick up the muck bucket. Annie was still there, leaning against the wall, a smile on her pretty face, arms crossed, studying him.

"You don't have to look at me that way."

"I don't?"

"I promised you I'd take your friend out."

"Her name is Martha."

"I agreed to take Martha out, and I will."

He trudged toward the house, aware that Annie was practically jogging to keep up with him.

"You're looking at this all wrong. It's not like an extra chore."

"So you say..."

"She's levelheaded and—"

He turned toward her so quickly that she nearly bumped into him. "And pretty. *Ya*, I heard."

"So what's the problem?"

"No problem, Annie." Instead of backing away, he stepped closer, causing her to cross her arms and frown at him. "Just be sure you keep up your end of the bargain."

"Of course."

"No more hiding your *dat*'s library books."

She pulled back in surprise.

"He's not that absentminded, and he wouldn't have left them on top of the washing machine where he found them."

"Oh, well... I might have been looking through them and..."

"Left them there by accident? Uh-huh. Just remember that we have a deal, and you have to keep your side of it if I'm going to keep mine."

When she'd nodded once, he turned and clomped into the house. He'd brought a map of Texas, and he was eager to show it to Alton. He'd even marked the route from Stephenville to Beeville. Sure, they were three hundred miles apart, but Levi wanted him to know that they wouldn't be completely alone in their new community.

By the time he'd had two cups of coffee, breakfast potatoes, eggs and pancakes, he was in a better mood. Alton had gone to find his reading glasses so he could better study the map. Lily was humming softly as she ran dishwater into the sink. And Annie?

Annie was throwing daggers his way, which was fine with him. She'd soon accept that there was no stopping him. He'd had his dreams trodden on by plenty of women before—girlfriends, his sisters, even his mother. Annie Kauffmann didn't represent that big of an obstacle. It was a shame, though. Her sort of stubborn spirit would have been a real asset in settling a new community.

Chapter Five

The first official meeting for those interested in a Texas community was held ten days later on a Friday afternoon. The weather was pleasant—still warm though it was now October. Storm clouds were building in the west. The front would bring rain and cooler temperatures, but Old Simon said it wouldn't hit before the next morning.

They'd placed chairs in the backyard in a semi-circle.

Levi had hoped half a dozen men would attend. He was pleasantly surprised when their numbers hit ten, including Jebediah and Alton.

There were three women, as well—Nicole, Jebediah's wife; Beth, who had married Avery the first Saturday Levi was in town; and Annie.

Marcus stood when it seemed everyone had arrived. "As your bishop, it's my duty to oversee any plans to split and/or begin a new community. I don't want to lose a single man, woman or child from our group. You're all vital to our church district here in Goshen, but I do want to be sensitive to *Gotte*'s leading. If it is *Gotte's wille* for you to begin a new life in Texas, then we will find a way to make it happen. These are, of course, the very early stages of inquiring and everyone here should understand that nothing has been decided. We'll move slowly, carefully and with consensus."

Marcus looked at Levi, who nodded in agreement.

They'd had this very talk the night before.

Marcus wasn't about to let any fool with a dream come in and disrupt his community, but at the same time he seemed like a fair man. And that was all that Levi could ask for. It was certainly more than he'd received from the community in Lancaster.

"How many families do you recommend we need?" Jebediah asked.

"Normally we suggest ten, at least. Since this community would be a good distance from any other—" Marcus held up his hand to stop Levi's protests. "Beeville is five hours away, by car, which you won't have and won't be able to afford to hire. Because there is a significant distance between you and another Plain community, I'm going to recommend that you have a firm commitment from a dozen to fifteen families before you purchase land."

Marcus studied the group and let the weight of what he was saying sink in. "You'll be on your own in Stephenville, and that's why it's important that you start with as much support from one another as possible. Also, I'm going to insist that you have at least three ministers so that you'll be able to hold proper church services."

Levi tried to stifle his groan, but with little success. He'd thought they would let the community begin with one minister, and he had that— Old Simon. Finding two more was not going to be easy.

"Any idea how we can find two more ministers?" Alton looked around at each person and then back at Marcus. "They're not exactly growing on trees."

The small joke went a long way to easing the tension in the group.

Avery Stutzman spoke for the first time since the meeting had begun. "We could put a notice in *The Budget* asking any interested persons, any interested ministers, to contact Levi or Marcus. I'd be happy to write that up and give it to our scribe. She could post it in the next issue."

Avery reached over and snagged his new bride's hand. "We're committed to helping make this happen. As a young newlywed couple..."

Beth and Avery smiled at each other and she blushed as the chuckles died down. "Having our own place is a real concern. My parents have land here, of course, as do Beth's parents. But we're both the youngest in our families, so there are a lot of siblings in line before us."

"We've been saving," Beth added. "But the cost of land here is a bit steeper than what we can afford at this point. At the rate things are going, it will be several years before we have our own place, and we'd rather not wait that long."

"It's a problem in nearly every Amish community." Marcus nodded in understanding. "As the group grows, as more people need and want to farm in an area, the price of land goes up. That's another thing to consider in a new community, as well. We need to do this carefully so the price per acre doesn't spike once the good folks in Texas realize we're coming."

At least that sounded more positive to Levi, though the deal about needing three ministers… it could be a problem. He didn't know if they'd be able to find two other men in leadership positions who would be willing and able to uproot their families.

It was decided that Marcus would contact bishops in neighboring communities and see if any of their ministers had a desire to help build a new group. Avery had volunteered to write a piece to give to their scribe, a girl named Naomi. Other persons attending vowed to write to relatives and friends in locations outside their county—looking for interested families as well as two additional ministers.

Levi had harbored high hopes for this meeting, but to this point, the news certainly wasn't all good. Of course it wasn't all bad, either. The folks assembled seemed eager and committed, for the most part.

It felt to Levi like they were taking two steps forward and one step back—but it was forward progress and that was all he could ask for. As the meeting progressed, his mood went from wildly optimistic to worried to cautiously hopeful. He was exhausted and ready to call it a night when Marcus asked for any last questions.

"I have a question."

He jerked toward the voice, sure it couldn't be...but it was. Pretty Annie Kauffmann had stood, squared her shoulders and faced the group. He had a bad feeling before she even tossed her question out.

"Why Texas?"

Levi had jumped up from his chair and was ready to blast a dozen reasons back her direction when Old Simon reached out, grasping his arm and pulling him back into a sitting position.

"But..."

Old Simon only shook his head and nodded toward Marcus who was listening intently to whatever Annie was saying. She spoke demurely and with a pleasant tone, as if she hadn't cooked up what she was going to say days ago.

Levi knew better.

This was a plot to ruin his chances of moving.

This was a scheme to keep her father in Goshen. Steam must have been shooting out of his ears, but he forced himself to focus in on her last words.

"I'm just wondering, why not Missouri or Arkansas? There's plenty of good farmland between here and Texas. Plus a community in Stephenville has been tried before, and it failed. So what has changed? Why do we think it will be successful now?"

Levi again tried to jump to his feet, but Old Simon's surprisingly strong grip on his arm held him back.

"Those are *gut* questions, Annie, and thank you for bringing them to our attention. In fact, if you hadn't, I would have." Marcus stared down at the sheet of paper where he'd jotted some notes. "I had planned to ask you all to carefully consider that very thing as you go about your work in the coming days. I beseech each of you to pray about this, seek *Gotte*'s guidance, and when we meet again in three weeks I'll ask Levi to address those very questions that Annie has brought to our attention."

The meeting broke up then, everyone stretching and talk turning to upcoming harvests, plans for winter crops and the fall festival which was to take place in a few weeks.

Levi saw Annie dart around the corner of the building. Fortunately her *dat* was still speaking with the bishop. Perfect. He'd have a few minutes alone with little miss Annie. Maybe she could explain why she was trying to sabotage his plans.

"Sabotage? You've got to be kidding."

"What would you call it?"

"Asking questions. I thought that's why we were meeting." Annie had guessed he wouldn't be happy with her, but she didn't think he'd have the nerve to follow her to the buggy.

"I don't even know why you're here." He waved his arms in the direction of Simon's backyard, nearly knocking off his hat. "Why would you bother coming to this meeting when you have no intention of moving with us?"

"I'm here because I care about what happens to my community, to my family."

"You care about them? Do you care if Avery and Beth are able to purchase land?"

"*Gotte* will provide a way."

"And maybe that way is moving to Texas!" Levi snatched his hat off his head and slapped it against his leg. "You wouldn't move if the entire community was packing up and leaving."

"And why should I? This is a *gut* place to live." She stomped her foot, which at first seemed to work because Levi stopped arguing with her, but then he shook his head and after that he started laughing. Before she could figure out what was so funny he was holding his side as if he had an ache from running.

"Do not laugh at me, Levi Lapp."

"I can't help it."

She stared at him in disbelief, so he held up his hands and repeated what he'd just said. "Honestly, I can't help it. Sorry. I'm sorry. You just look so… well, funny."

"I look *funny*?"

"I want to stay mad at you. I still am mad at you. I'm plenty steamed, but if you could see the look on your face…and then you stomped your foot like some child annoyed at not getting your way."

"Did you just call me a child?"

"I said *like* a child—not the same thing."

He moved to her buggy and rested his back against it, his hands still pressed against his stomach, his gaze on the ground. "You are one interesting gal, Annie Kauffmann."

"What's that supposed to mean?"

"You have no problem speaking your mind."

"Why should I?"

"Not exactly the meek Amish woman pictured in romance novels."

"What do you know about romance novels?"

"My *schweschdern* kept them around the house… I used to tease them about it."

It was the first time Levi had mentioned his family, and Annie felt her anger toward him soften.

"Don't you miss them?"

"Some."

"Then why—"

His look silenced her. Okay. Not a subject he wanted to talk about. That was fine with her.

"We had a deal," he reminded her.

"I haven't tried to stop you from talking to my *dat*."

"But you came to this meeting when you obviously have no intention of moving."

"It doesn't hurt to know the status of things, and I'd rather receive my information firsthand than hear it from the grapevine."

"Okay, fair enough. Come and listen."

"I wasn't asking for your permission."

"And I didn't mean it that way."

He stared at the ground a moment before raising those gorgeous blue eyes to study her. He really was a nice-looking guy.

"But do you have to throw out obstructive questions?"

"Obstructive? Someone was paying attention in English class."

"Look me in the eye and tell me that you were not trying to throw down a roadblock."

She squirmed under his gaze and finally admitted, "Yes and no."

"I understand the yes part of that answer."

"I'll admit, you all looked like a bunch of starstruck fools—so, yes, I was trying to splash some cold water on the group."

"Finally, some honesty."

"But also no—because I didn't ask *why Texas* for the sole purpose of slowing your progress."

"Okay, then, explain it to me."

"I honestly want to know." Her hands went to her hips again, and a smile twitched on Levi's lips. It made her want to stomp her foot once more but she resisted. No need sending him into more gales of laughter. "Why Texas, Levi?"

He didn't answer her right away.

The people who had attended the meeting were walking around the corner of the house now. A few saw them and waved. Great. Now they'd think she was stepping out with Levi Lapp.

"Maybe I should have addressed that to begin

with. You were correct when you pointed out that there are other places—closer places—we could move. Missouri and Arkansas are both *gut* examples, and I've been to communities in both of them."

"Let me guess. They don't measure up to your memories of Texas."

"They're *gut* places, I guess. Pretty much like Indiana. Arkansas has more mountains—a different way of life than what we have here. Missouri has plenty of farmland, and we would basically be living the life we have here in a different state. Maybe costs are less. I'm not really sure. I guess I'll be checking before our next meeting."

"Information isn't a bad thing, Levi."

"Sure. I understand."

"But…"

"But, they're not Texas, and that's something that you can't understand unless you've been there." He resettled his ridiculous hat on his head and pushed away from the buggy. When he turned back toward her the laughing friend was gone and the adversary was back—but it seemed to be a kinder, gentler adversary.

"I've been there, Annie, and it's my life dream to go back. I only hope that I have that opportunity. Did you know that Texas comes from the Native American word for friend or ally?" And without any further explanation, he turned back toward the house, shoulders slightly bowed from the weight of the task before him.

In that moment, Annie experienced a sudden and profound remorse. She'd pulled the rug out from under his feet, and although she didn't regret that, she hated to see him so dejected.

"Martha enjoyed going out for ice cream with you."

He stopped, turned and nodded once. Then he walked back toward the house without another word.

Martha had told Annie earlier that day that she'd enjoyed the trip for ice cream and the walk down the Pumpkinvine Trail. She'd gone alone with Levi on the first date, but Levi had suggested they bring Big Tom along on the second. They'd ended up eating snow cones—she'd had grape, Big Tom had cherry and Levi had settled for coconut.

"I told you I thought he was a nice guy," Annie had said.

"*Ya*, I know. The thing is…he did more than tolerate Big Tom. He actually included him."

But it was the last thing Martha had said that had stuck in Annie's mind, that she replayed over and over as she'd tried to sleep the night before. "Some people don't make *gut* couples because they're complete opposites. Levi and I would never be right for one another because we're too much alike."

Levi was like her best friend? How was that even possible?

And why did the thought of that deepen her remorse and cause her to wonder if she should be fighting Levi's plan at all? Because she still didn't want to move to Texas, and she still planned to do everything in her ability to stop her family from doing so.

The only difference was now she felt bad about it.

Annie woke the next Wednesday determined to shake her foul mood.

As she pulled out her most worn dress, she vowed not to care that Levi had taken Martha on another date—after all, she'd asked him to, hadn't she?

Fastening a frayed *kapp* to her head she stared at herself in the mirror and scolded her image. It was time to stop dwelling on the look of hurt on Levi's face when she'd thrown cold water on his plans at the meeting. Her questions had been good ones. If settling in Stephenville, Texas, didn't work before, why would it work now? And why there? Despite what Levi thought, there were bound to be good places closer to Goshen.

Pulling on her work boots, she remembered

how she'd stomped her foot at him and he'd laughed—laughed at her when she was trying to make a point. If he'd been angry, it would have been more satisfying, but to have him laugh at her? That was just insulting.

She fastened a stained but clean apron around her dress and marched down the stairs. The rain had held off, though cooler temperatures had arrived. She actually needed a sweater or shawl in the evenings. Her *dat* had informed the family that the corn harvest would begin today. Harvesting was always a family affair and two of her *bruders* would be there to help. Her oldest *schweschder* would arrive in time to help Mamm fix a big lunch. It would be a busy day filled with hard work, good food and family.

She stomped into the kitchen refusing to let the fact that Levi Lapp would be in the middle of it all ruin her mood.

It took some effort, but she held on to her complaints through breakfast and cleaning the dishes. Once she stepped outside, though—into a fall day that had dawned crisp and clear—even she couldn't help smiling.

"That's my girl," Mamm said.

So she'd noticed.

Of course she'd noticed, but her parents believed a bad mood had to be worked through on a private level. Annie didn't have them often, and they usually blew over quickly, so perhaps her parents were right.

But honestly, who could be angry when surrounded by so many of God's blessings? That would be worse than stubborn. It would be ungrateful, and Annie couldn't find it in her heart to be that.

So she smiled at her *mamm*, bounded down the steps and hurried out to the field.

Nathan and Joseph had eaten an early breakfast at home, but they were already standing by her *dat* next to the field where the corn waited to be harvested. Even the horses seemed eager to begin their work.

The sun was barely peeking over the horizon and the weather was cool. Finally, fall was here. And fall in Indiana was a special time indeed.

The stalks had been cut and stacked into tepees two weeks before. Now they were sufficiently dry to separate the corn from the husks. It would take everyone working all day to finish the job, and she'd be working side by side with Levi.

"*Gude mariye*," he said as she walked up to join the group.

She was about to answer when her father raised his hand for quiet.

"Nathan and Joe, I want you working collecting. Levi and I will stand on the wagon and catch and stack. Annie, you'll drive. Now let's take a moment to pray that *Gotte* blesses our harvest and keeps each of us safely in the palm of his hand."

There were times when Annie wished they prayed aloud, where she could simply listen to the calming sound of her *dat*'s voice. Instead the silence forced her to speak to *Gotte*. She found herself confessing her ungratefulness, her tendency to consider her wants and needs more important than those of others, her love for her family and this day and their simple life.

After her father said, "And in His name, we pray…" and everyone answered "Amen," Levi glanced her way.

Did he just wink at her?

Annie looked at the ground, back at the house and then at Levi who was smiling broadly.

They walked together toward the wagon that was already hitched to the Percherons. Pop was the older of the two. He had a light gray coat, stood sixteen hands tall and weighed nearly two thousand pounds. Annie reached in her pocket and handed him a carrot.

"I was a toddler when Dat bought Pop. He's older, but still strong, still a *gut* workhorse."

"I've cleaned out their stalls for nearly a month now, but I haven't really spent any time with them." Levi ran his hand down the neck of the other workhorse. He was chestnut colored and nearly identical in size to Pop.

"That's Pretty Boy. We've only had him three years now."

"You'll drive careful, right?"

"I always do."

"You won't intentionally knock me off?"

"How can you even suggest such a thing?"

"It's no secret I'm like a burr under your saddle."

"We don't have saddles. We're Amish." How many times had she reminded him? This time instead of being irritated at her correction, he smiled even more broadly.

"Just remember your *dat* is riding back there with me."

He held out a hand to help boost her up onto the wagon bench seat.

She ignored it, grabbed the handle and pulled herself up.

And then they were harvesting, and she didn't spend another minute arguing with Levi Lapp in her mind. She was too busy minding Pop and Pretty Boy.

Enjoying the sounds of her brothers as they pulled the corncobs from the husks and tossed them to the wagon.

Even smiling when Levi and Dat picked up the chorus of "I Have Decided" and then followed it with "Victory in Jesus" and "Will the Circle Be Unbroken." The morning flew by, and she was surprised when the sound of her mother ringing the dinner bell echoed across the field.

Nathan jumped up onto the wagon, reminding her of the young teen he'd once been. Now he was thirty and had seven children of his own. "I'll take them to the barn."

"Are you sure?"

"Can't have my little *schweschder* watering horses."

She handed him the reins and stepped down, dismayed to see Levi waiting for her. Her father and Joseph were already walking toward the house.

"You didn't have to wait."

"I wanted to."

She started to ask why, but she didn't want to ruin her good mood by being snarky.

"You're pretty *gut* with the horses."

"Danki." She fished around for something else to say. Why did she suddenly feel tongue-tied around Levi Lapp? It occurred to her that he was adorable in a lost puppy kind of way.

"You're smiling."

"I am?"

Instead of answering, he bumped his shoulder against hers. They walked toward the house where she could see her *mamm* and oldest sister, Mary, had set lunch out on the picnic table beneath the maple trees. The sight brought a cascade of memories to her mind—twenty-four years' worth, though she wasn't certain she could remember the early ones.

But always they'd had the fall harvest.

Always family had helped.

Always they'd had lunch under these trees.

She glanced at Levi, saw a smile spread across his face as he looked at the spread of food and gathering of her family.

"It's *gut* here," she said. "This place? This land? It's *gut*."

He slowed and studied her for a moment, and Annie had the ridiculous notion that he was about to reach for her hand. Instead, Levi again nudged her shoulder and said, "I'll race you."

Which was completely ridiculous. After all, they were not *kinner* anymore. Laughter bubbled out of her, sounding young and hopeful and free. And then she was running to catch up, because she couldn't stand the thought of Levi Lapp beating her even at something as silly as a race to the lunch table.

Chapter Six

Levi had expected to like Annie's family from the very beginning, but he hadn't expected to feel so comfortable with them. He pushed back from the table, certain that if he ate another bite he'd be asleep in the field rather than working in it.

"I think I better walk this off," he muttered and headed toward the shady side of the lawn. He was surprised when Joseph walked out of the barn and joined him.

"Ready for the second shift?"

Levi patted his stomach. "The mind is willing, but…"

"*Ya.* The flesh is full."

"Indeed."

"Dat always takes a thirty-minute break after the meal is done. You'd think we were going out to swim instead of harvest." Joseph pushed his hat back on his head.

Levi thought of Annie making fun of his hat, and then it occurred to him how he and Joseph must look. Both Amish. Both relatively young men. One traditionally Amish, wearing the customary straw hat, and the other—him—not so traditional, wearing his Stetson. They were both standing at the fence, hands crossed over the top bar, watching the workhorses nod in the sun. In that moment, he felt their similarities outweighed their differences. He felt, temporarily at least, like a part of something bigger than himself.

"Actually what I wanted to talk to you about was Annie."

"Annie?"

"We're all a bit protective of her."

"*Bruders* usually are." He'd felt that way toward his own *schweschdern* once. Then they'd grown up, married and decided it was their job to set him straight.

"It's what I wanted to talk to you about."

Levi looked at him in surprise.

"It's obvious that you like her."

"Annie? I like her fine."

"You're not understanding what I'm trying to say. It's *obvious* that you're interested in her."

"Annie?" His voice screeched like when he was a *youngie* and everything was changing. He swallowed, took a deep breath and forced himself to speak in a normal voice. "*Nein*, not like that. She can barely tolerate being around me."

"That's not what it looks like from where I'm standing."

Levi glanced back toward the picnic area. The women were cleaning up, and Annie was in the middle of them stacking dishes into a tub.

"Maybe you need glasses then..." Levi's words trailed off as he thought of Annie working in her wedding trailer, Annie driving the horses, Annie running beside him across the field.

Joseph cleared his throat, and Levi forced his attention back to the conversation. "As far as Annie is concerned, you've got the wrong guy, or something."

"So you don't have romantic feelings for my little *schweschder*?"

Levi opened his mouth, closed it, opened it again. He felt like a fish out of water. He felt completely disoriented.

"Just be careful. Annie's the youngest in our family, as you know, so we all feel as if we need to look out for her."

"You have nothing to worry about with me. She doesn't...she can't even stand...you've got this all wrong."

Joseph patted him on the shoulder. "Maybe you don't realize how you feel at this point."

"And you do?"

"I'm asking you to be mindful of how you treat her. If you don't plan on staying—and from what I've heard from Dat, you don't—then it's probably best to not even go that direction with her."

"But if Alton and Lily move, then—"

"My parents moving would be difficult for her, but does that mean she will too? Not likely." Joseph crossed his arms, studying the scene before them. The fields, the picnic, the family—it could be an illustration for a book on Amish life. "Annie's always had an independent spirit. She worked hard to build up a *gut* business, and she probably won't give it up even when she marries, though she'll have to cut back some or hire other workers to help her. But moving to Texas? I don't see that happening even if Dat and Mamm go."

Joseph resettled his hat on his head. "So I'd appreciate you not leading her on." With those words, he walked away.

Suddenly Levi understood what had puzzled him since his arrival. He understood as clearly as if it had been carved on a tablet and handed to him.

He wasn't merely suggesting a move to her parents. If what he hoped would happen did happen, then Annie's entire world would be turned on its head.

* * *

Annie saw Joseph talking to Levi. She hoped it had been about the harvest, or church or even the community he'd come from. Worst-case scenario, he was asking questions about Texas, but she didn't see that happening. Joseph had a very prosperous farm as well as a woodworking business. She couldn't see him starting over again somewhere else, especially with such a large family.

But maybe she was wrong.

Maybe he was already worried about land for his sons.

Possibly Texas sounded like the promised land to him same as it did to Levi.

The thought filled her with dread. Would she lose her entire family to Levi's dream? She pushed the thought away, determined not to let her worries ruin such a beautiful fall day.

The afternoon passed even more quickly than the morning had. She spent two hours on the back of the wagon, catching and stacking corn, another hour walking along the rows and pulling the cobs from the shucks and the final two hours driving the team.

By the time her *dat* called it a day, she was so dead on her feet that sleeping in the field seemed like a valid option.

"Tired?" Levi asked.

"How can you tell?"

"Because you're standing still staring at the house instead of walking toward it."

She glanced at him, exasperated to see that he had enough energy to tease her. Annie sighed and began plodding toward the house, and Levi matched her step for step. If she was going to have to walk with him, she might as well ask what was on her mind.

"What were you talking to Joseph about?"

"Joseph?"

"My *bruder.* The guy you stood with outside the barn after lunch."

"I know who he is."

"So what were you talking to him about? Please tell me it was not about Texas."

"Nein." His answer was soft and he avoided looking directly at her.

She didn't think he would lie to her, but something was up.

"Then what were you talking about?"

"Oh…" Levi seemed to hesitate. When had he ever minced words before? Finally, he plunged ahead. "Joseph was warning me that they're protective of you."

"Protective?" They were halfway across the field. She could see her father releasing the horses into the pasture, Nathan forking hay into the feeder and Joseph pouring water from the horse trough over his head. "Protective how?"

Levi jerked the hat off his head, and that was when she noticed how red his ears were. Had he somehow sunburned them, or…

"They think that we're interested in one another—romantically."

Her mouth fell open. She tried to think of how to respond to that, but her thoughts were suddenly spinning in a dozen directions at the same time. She shook her head and snapped her mouth shut, though she continued to stare at him.

"I know."

"You know what?"

"That the notion is ludicrous. You can barely stand to be around me."

"That's not true."

"My hat irritates you." He waved the Stetson. "It's not Amish."

"My boots irritate you."

"They're cowboy boots."

"And my dream of moving to Texas irritates you."

The look he gave her reminded Annie of a child who had been scolded.

"It's not your dream that bothers me, Levi."

"It's how it will affect your family. I know. I understand that now."

"You do?"

He nodded, slapped the Stetson against his leg releasing a small cloud of dust and positioned it back on his head. "And I'm sorry."

"You're sorry?" She could hear herself repeating his words like some sort of well-trained parrot, but she couldn't seem to stop. "You're sorry?"

"I am, Annie." His tone of voice, his posture, even his expression told her that he was no longer teasing. He was serious. Levi Lapp was seriously apologizing for disrupting her life and sending her future plans into a tailspin.

She hadn't seen that coming.

How should she respond?

She had no idea. So she resumed walking toward the house.

"I was so focused on what I wanted, that it never occurred to me how it would affect you. When I came here, I only knew Old Simon. I certainly didn't anticipate meeting your family."

"And yet you were looking for families just like mine."

"I was. That's true, but maybe…maybe I should have backed off when I saw how much it upset you. Instead, I dug in deeper."

Her voice dropped, an image popping in her mind from her childhood. "There are times you remind me of our old hound dog whenever he found a bone."

They were nearly to the house. He put a hand

on her arm and didn't remove it until she'd stopped and turned to face him. "I don't know how I'm going to fix this, but I promise you that I will try."

He waited a moment, maybe to see if she believed him, maybe to wait for her response which never came because she still had no idea what to say.

Then he turned and trudged toward the barn, and Annie was left trying to figure out what had just happened.

Annie thought of trying to set her family straight. But everything she came up with sounded like a *youngie* protesting that she didn't have a crush when she did. Instead, she vowed to keep quiet on the topic. She washed up, changed clothes and made it downstairs as her *mamm* was putting dinner on the table. Joseph and Nathan had headed home to eat with their own families. Mary had helped prepare the meal and then hurried home as well. As they settled around the table it was only Annie, her parents and Levi.

She expected things to be uncomfortable, and indeed, at least three different times, she caught her parents sending each other silent looks. They'd done that as long as she could remember. It was as if they had their own wordless communication system. Was that what it was like to be married? To be able to know what your spouse was thinking without uttering a word? Annie wasn't sure she was ready for that kind of intimacy. The idea that her family thought she wanted such a relationship with Levi Lapp almost caused her to laugh out loud.

"Levi, you were a big help today." Her *dat* reached for a second helping of potato casserole.

"*Danki.* I enjoy harvest, always have."

"You haven't talked much about your family other than to mention they're in Lancaster."

Annie fought the urge to roll her eyes. She'd been through this before—once when she was dating a boy from Shipshewana and another time when she'd stepped out with a boy who had recently moved to Goshen. It was as if her *dat* had a list of questions for any prospective beaus.

She barely heard Levi's reply. She was too busy trying to think of a way to derail her parents' confused ideas about her and Levi.

Her *dat* continued to pepper him with questions about Lancaster. Bits and pieces of Levi's responses registered: sixty-five-acre farm, a few dairy cows, all the children grown and gone but an oldest brother living on the family farm.

Her *mamm* wanted to know how many siblings he had—two sisters who were older than Levi and two younger half sisters. Annie dropped her fork and stared at him at the mention of a stepfather.

"My *dat* died when I was fifteen," Levi explained. "We were living here in Goshen at the time, and then my *mamm* remarried. Not too long after that we moved."

Annie's *mamm* carefully pressed her napkin to her lips and then folded it in her lap. "I'm sorry, Levi. I don't believe I knew your parents. I guess even then Goshen was large enough to have divided into several church districts."

"*Ya*, we lived a *gut* ways from here, what I can remember of it."

"We are all sorry for your loss." Her *dat* echoed her *mamm*'s sentiment. "Couldn't have been easy for a young man to lose his father."

Levi shrugged and changed the subject, asking when they'd begin to plant the winter wheat. Soon they were deep into a discussion on crop rotation.

Annie stood to help clean the dishes, but her mother made up a bogus excuse for Annie to see Levi out.

"They've done this before," she said as she walked him toward the barn.

"Done what?"

"Decided that I'm interested in someone, and gone out of their way to be accommodating." She tried to laugh, but really it was humiliating. She didn't need her parents' help to find a beau.

"They care about you."

"*Ya*, but they also think they know what's best."

"Don't all parents? Mine certainly thought they knew what was best for me—staying in Lancaster, farming a tiny place because that's all we could afford, starting a side business to support the farm. It's what my stepdad had done and what my brothers-in-law had done. They were convinced I should stay and do the same." Levi shook his head. "They couldn't grasp the idea that the life I wanted was different from the one they had."

"I understand firsthand how frustrating that is. Mamm and Dat have been supportive of my business, but I think at first they were convinced it was a phase I'd grow out of."

"Plainly they are proud of you."

"And plainly they want me married." Her cheeks burned even saying the words. At least it was dark and Levi couldn't see.

She helped him hitch Old Simon's horse to his buggy.

"He's had this mare as long as I can remember." The mare was black with white socks. Annie stepped closer and rubbed her hand up and down the horse's neck. "Old Simon's wife named her."

"First mare I've ever known named after a flower."

"Petunia's a *gut* name. Tabitha named the milk cows too—Rosebud and Daisy and Tulip."

Levi started laughing. "You're making that up."

"I'm not."

Instead of climbing up into the buggy, Levi turned around, his back against the buggy, and stared up at the stars.

"Please don't tell me the stars are brighter in Texas."

He didn't. Instead he began to sing "Deep in the Heart of Texas." She'd heard it before. But she'd heard it as an energetic children's song that they'd sung in school when they were learning about each state.

Levi sang it like a lullaby, and for the first time Annie found herself curious about this state that had captured his heart.

She moved beside him, stared up at the sky and wondered if it could be true. Were the stars brighter in Texas? She didn't ask. She didn't want to know.

Levi nudged his shoulder against hers. "I've figured out what we should do."

"About what?" Annie was distracted by Levi's closeness. She wondered what it would be like to kiss him.

"About your family."

"Oh, *ya*. Tell me. I'm all ears. Because trying to persuade them something isn't so only convinces them that it is."

"So we should do it."

"Do it?"

"Step out together."

She squinted at him in the darkness, trying to make out his expression. Finally, she found her voice. "Did you hit your head today? Stay out in the sun too long? Maybe you're having a small stroke?"

"Why is it such a crazy idea?"

"Well…we're complete opposites."

"True."

"You're not going to be here very long if your plan works."

"I didn't ask you to marry me."

"And I didn't ask you to ask me."

Instead of becoming exasperated with her, which he had every right to be, Levi began to laugh.

"See?" He stuck his thumbs inside his suspenders. "This is what I enjoy about us."

"There is no *us*."

"You never say what I expect, and you always say what's on your mind."

"Not always."

He laughed again, as if she'd said something very witty. She was beginning to wonder if he was a little daft, but then his tone grew serious.

"Joseph warned me not to mislead you, but we're being honest with one another here. I know you're not really interested in me." He said it as if he were relating the weather forecast. "Your parents plainly want us to step out, so we'll do it, and then…"

"Then what?"

"I don't know. Show them that we're incompatible, I guess."

She wound her *kapp* string around her finger. "What about Martha?"

Levi shook his head. "I've told you. There's nothing between me and Martha. She's like a nicer, kinder version of my little *schweschder*."

Martha had said practically the same thing about Levi to Annie the day before, but she hadn't believed her. Why did she feel such a sense of relief hearing Levi confirm it? Why did she even care?

Instead of pointing out how ridiculous their plan was, she found herself saying, "It might work."

"Really?"

"I mean it might prove to my parents that we're mismatched. We can step out a few times, and then when it's obvious we don't belong together—"

"Plainly, we don't."

"Then we can say we tried, and they'll back off. This isn't the first time they've poked their collective noses in my social life. And don't say it. I know. They care about me."

"It's a deal then."

He'd climbed up in the buggy, but he leaned back down and said, "I still want to go to Texas, still plan to. I'm going to find a way."

"I'm sure you will."

"But I've mucked things up for you, and I'm going to find a way to undo that."

"You mean with Dat?"

"And your *bruder* Jebediah. Why wasn't he here today?"

"Had to get his own corn up, though his crop was much smaller and he was able to do it with the help of a neighbor. You know how it is—everyone harvests at the same time."

Levi stared out over the mare, out toward the fields they'd just harvested. "You have a nice life here. I can see that now. My future—it's to the south, but my dream doesn't have to be your *dat*'s."

"Maybe you could mention some of the bad things about Texas."

"I'll have to be a little more subtle than that, but I'll think of something." He turned to look at her then. "I promise."

He waited until she nodded, then he picked up the reins, released the brake and guided Petunia down their lane. It occurred to her that Levi Lapp was a good man, and he'd make some Amish girl a fine husband.

* * *

Levi didn't expect Old Simon to still be up when he finally made it into the house. The drive from Annie's was only ten minutes, and he often walked. Since he knew they'd be working later and he'd be staying for dinner, he'd taken the buggy. Plus, Simon rarely took it out alone anymore. Levi didn't hurry as he unhitched the buggy and cared for the horse. Those things calmed him, helped him to process all that had happened. By the time he stepped into the sitting room, it was well past the old guy's normal bedtime.

But there he sat, in his rocker, whittling on a cane.

He carved crosses into the tops of them, sanded them until they were as smooth as the softest cotton and sold them at a store in town. It was a way to earn extra money, but more than that it was something he seemed to enjoy doing.

"How was the harvest?"

Levi sank onto the couch and told him about the day in the field.

When he'd finished, Simon said, "Sounds as if our Annie has caught your fancy."

"Why do you say that?"

"Because you mentioned her quite a bit, but hardly spoke at all about her *bruders*."

"Oh, her *bruders* seem like nice people too."

Simon smiled, but he didn't comment on that. Realizing that he would hear about his and Annie's dating, Levi decided to tell him about it before someone else could.

"Actually, we're going to be stepping out together—Annie and I."

"Thought you were seeing the Weaver girl."

"*Ya*, I was, but we decided…that is, it seems like…well, what I mean is, we're *freinden,* is all."

"Love often starts as friendship."

Did it ever start as enemies? The question almost popped out of Levi's mouth, but he managed to rein it in. He and Annie hadn't been adversaries—not exactly. That was too harsh a word. It was true that they were on opposite sides of the Texas issue, but now he understood why. It didn't weaken his resolve to move there. In fact, he realized, in that moment, that he felt less anxious than he had since moving to Goshen. It no longer seemed that Annie was working against him, only that they were on separate paths.

"She's a *gut* girl, our Annie." Simon ran a hand up and down the walking stick checking for rough spots. "Seems as if only yesterday she was a young thing, running around with the *kinner*."

"Not many Amish women run their own business."

As soon as he uttered the words, Levi remembered Annie admonishing him about how many

Amish women did work to help the family budget—bakers, quilters, etc. She'd been right. He'd simply never taken the time to think about it.

But what she'd done?

The wedding trailer?

Cooking for hundreds of people at a time? *Nein.* There weren't many women that he knew who could accomplish such a thing.

"It's true," Simon said. "But Annie saw a need in our community and met it."

"Because Goshen has grown so much."

"That—and also because now Amish women are busier than ever." Simon added a touch of oil to his rag and proceeded to rub it into the cane. "Raising a household of children, keeping the house and preparing the meals—those things are a tremendous amount of work. Plus, most families now have cottage businesses that are important to their livelihood. Unfortunately it's become harder and harder to make it on farming alone."

It occurred to Levi that Simon's thinking was remarkably clear tonight. There was none of the confusion he'd witnessed earlier. Hadn't he mixed up the Red River with the Mississippi just the day before? Perhaps his confusion only happened when he was tired or stressed.

"I agree that times are hard—even for an Amish farmer who is supposed to be self-sufficient. The cost of land is so prohibitive. It's why I want to start a community in Texas."

"*Ya.* Sure and certain it could be less expensive there, if you pick the right spot. But farming is always hard, Levi, especially dry-land farming."

"I didn't claim it wasn't." He felt the old defensiveness rise up in him—like a cat being stroked the wrong way.

"I knew you were aware. We've lived there— you and I have. You were old enough when we left to know that the farming was difficult—it wasn't all bluebonnets and rodeos."

"Are you against the idea of moving?"

"Not at all." Simon ran the rag over the cane one last time, then stood and carried it to a corner of the room where he placed it with the ones that were ready to go to town. "But I wouldn't want to misrepresent what we're doing. We're not going to the promised land, though it might appear that way from a distance."

"I'm aware."

"We work and toil in this life, live simply, try to be a good neighbor and follow *Gotte's* word. Rest assured, you'll face challenges in Texas same as here. Let's be very certain that everyone understands that."

Levi wanted to take offense at the words. It felt like the old guy was lecturing him, but a crack had opened in Levi's dreams and the smallest bit of doubt had crept in.

Was he only remembering the best parts of Texas?

Had he forgotten how difficult it was living there?

And worse yet, what if Annie was right? What if there was somewhere closer, somewhere better, that he hadn't considered? Not only would he be risking the money he'd saved, but he'd be leading a group of people right off the proverbial cliff with him.

Chapter Seven

Annie was busy on Thursday—from the moment the sun rose until it settled in the west. She barely had a moment to rest what with catching up on the household chores and setting things straight in the wedding trailer.

By Friday morning, she felt that she'd made up for the day she'd lost harvesting. As she drank coffee with her *mamm*, she made a long list of things she needed to purchase. Although Priscilla bought most of their food in bulk at the local big-box discount store, there were still items she needed to pick up at local stores.

And there was another reason she was eager to take the buggy out. On the way to town, she had to pass right by Martha's place. No harm in stopping to see if she'd like to ride along.

Her *mamm* thought it was a fine plan and added a few things she needed to the bottom of Annie's list. After they'd had breakfast and cleaned up the dishes, her *dat* brought the buggy around. She couldn't help smiling when she walked up to Bella. They'd bought the mare four years ago, but Annie still thought she was the prettiest buggy mare she'd ever seen—chestnut colored with three white socks and a sweet disposition.

She headed off to town feeling fairly optimistic about the day, though she dreaded confronting Martha. "Not a confrontation," she tried to assure herself. "More like an informational meeting."

Big Tom was off with one of his *bruders*, looking at goats.

"He's quite excited," Martha said. "We had some, years ago, and he's forgotten how much trouble they can be."

"My *dat* says if water can get through a fence, a goat can and will."

"*Ya*, I've heard that one. There's some truth to it too."

Martha was keen on spending a few hours away from the farm. They stopped by the fabric store where Annie purchased several yards of lace that she planned to use on her centerpieces the next day. Then they went to the general store for the rest of the items on her list. By the time they were finished there, Annie realized she'd skipped lunch and was starving.

"Coffee and a treat?"

"You'll never hear me turn down either of those things."

Annie ordered coffee and a cranberry-walnut scone. Martha chose coffee and a large blueberry muffin. When they sat down, both girls cut their treat in half and swapped. It was something they'd done since they were young. They didn't even think about it anymore—best friends shared, and Martha certainly was her best friend.

It was after they'd finished their food and were sipping on refills of coffee that Annie brought up the subject of Levi. She explained how he'd helped with the harvest, how her family had misinterpreted their friendship and what they'd decided to do about it.

By the time she was done, Martha was grinning like a child who'd caught her first fish.

"Why are you looking at me that way?"

"What way?"

"As if you expected this."

"But I did expect this."

Annie stared at Martha. She wasn't offended exactly, more surprised. Martha had always been the more insightful one, while Annie had always been the one to jump into action. Still, she hadn't seen this coming at all.

"It's not real," she reminded her.

"Uh-huh."

"We're not truly interested in each other."

"So you mentioned—at least three times now."

"It's just that my parents are quite single-minded. You know how they are. Once they get an idea in their heads, it's impossible to convince them it isn't so..." The rest of her explanation died on her lips when she saw Martha was now outright laughing at her, though she was attempting to hide it behind her napkin.

"What?"

"Maybe you don't realize that Levi is quite taken with you."

"Taken with me?"

"That's what I said."

"Now you're being *narrisch*."

"I'm perfectly sane and you know it."

"Then why would you suggest such a thing?"

"Because it's true."

"Definitely is not true."

"I've spent a lot of time with him the last few weeks, thanks to the elaborate plan you concocted."

"Desperate more than elaborate."

"He talks about you all the time."

"What?" Her voice had climbed an octave and an older *Englisch* couple turned their direction, eyebrows raised. Annie forced her voice down. "What are you talking about?"

"Always it was Annie this and Annie that. He's

quite smitten with you and probably doesn't even know it."

"Martha Weaver. I believe you're teasing me."

"I'm not." She leaned forward and dropped her voice to a whisper. "One day he even told me that you would make a fine *fraa*…"

"He said that? About me?"

"Uh-huh."

"What else did he say? I can tell you're holding something back."

"*Nein*, I'm not."

"Spill it."

"Well, okay. He said you'd make a fine *fraa* for someone who didn't mind an opinionated, stubborn and very strong-willed woman."

"See?" Annie sat back, satisfied that she hadn't misread the situation. "That sounds more like the Levi I know."

"If you say so. It's a little warm in here. Are you ready to go? I think I need some fresh air."

The day was drizzly, but they'd stopped by the library earlier, and she'd checked the weather on the computer. The forecast promised things would clear off during the late afternoon. Tomorrow should be sunny but crisp—perfect weather for a wedding.

She pulled in a deep breath as Martha joined her on the sidewalk, linked their arms together, and turned them toward the buggy.

Martha's voice was suddenly serious. "It's okay, you know. If you like him."

"Because you two are just *freinden*."

"Yup."

"Because you're so much alike."

"Exactly."

"I'm going to disagree with that. You're kind and giving and compassionate…"

"If you could have seen Levi with Big Tom, you'd understand that he is those things too."

"All right. I'm not saying he doesn't have *gut* qualities, but he's also more bullheaded than those Texas longhorns he's always bragging about."

"Not always a bad thing."

They'd reached the buggy. Annie fed a carrot to Bella, patting the mare and thanking her for waiting so patiently. When they were settled inside, and Annie had set the mare into a nice trot down the street, Martha said what was on her mind, what she'd probably been trying to say from the beginning.

"It's okay if you change your mind about a thing or a person. Sometimes first impressions aren't the best. Sometimes we have to see past that impression to the scars and hopes and dreams underneath, and then we understand who they really are."

"And you think that's what is happening between Levi and me?"

"Maybe."

"I don't know. Honestly when I think about Levi, my thoughts and feelings are a jumble."

"Give it time, my friend. But please, keep an open mind."

Could she do that where Levi was concerned? And did she owe it to Levi to give him a fresh start? She hadn't made the best first impression, either. She could still remember the lecture she'd given him that first night he'd had dinner at her parents' house.

So what was she supposed to do?

See past Levi's scars, as Martha had suggested?

How did a person even do that?

She puzzled over that question long after she'd dropped off Martha at her place. She was nearly back home before it occurred to her that maybe this wasn't something that she could figure out on her own. Maybe it was something she needed to pray about.

Levi kept trying to find time to speak with Annie on Sunday, but either she was extraordinarily busy or she was avoiding him. There was no church meeting that day. Instead, it was a visiting Sunday, and he and Old Simon had been invited to eat with Annie's family. The place was starting to feel very familiar to him. It was starting to feel more like home than his mother and stepfather's place ever had.

He drove Petunia right up to the barn and released her into the adjacent field as Old Simon made his way over to the luncheon tables.

Unfortunately it wasn't the quiet, intimate affair he'd hoped for. It seemed that all of Annie's family were there—two older *bruders*, two older *schweschdern*, all their spouses and plenty of nieces and nephews. He gave up trying to remember all the children's names.

For reasons he couldn't fathom, Annie was in a state of constant motion. She was the last to sit down to eat—taking a place at the opposite end of the table from him—and the first to jump up and start clearing dishes. It was possible she was avoiding him.

The thought bothered him more than he wanted it to. He wanted not to care. It wasn't like she'd confessed her affection for him, but they had come up with a plan. He'd thought he was helping her out. Now he wasn't so sure.

Clouds had been building through the morning, so it was no surprise when the sky darkened even more and a gentle, soaking rain began to fall. The adults sought refuge on the wraparound covered porch. The children headed to the barn. After confirming that Annie wasn't on the porch, he darted across the yard, soaking his clothes in the process. It was worth getting wet because the minute he stepped into the barn he found her.

She looked as pretty as she had bustling around the table, but now her eyes were covered with a checkered dishcloth that had been folded into a rectangle and tied around her head. She held out her arms to keep from walking into anything, and a bright smile covered her face. The children called out to her as she sought to tag them.

"Can't catch me."

"You're not even close."

"This could take days."

Before he realized what had happened, she'd banged an arm against his chest and shouted "Ha! You're It." The expression on her face when she yanked off the blindfold and saw who she'd tagged was priceless.

"Where did you come from?"

"Outside. It's raining."

"*Ya.* I know. That's why we're in here." Her face was flushed and she was twirling the blindfold in her hands.

If he'd thought he would have time to talk to her, he was sadly mistaken. They were surrounded by kids. It seemed as if the number had doubled since lunch and they were all shouting, "You're It, Levi. She tagged you!"

It should have been a simple game.

One he hadn't played in many years.

Still, it was embarrassing that it took him so long to tag someone. He kept hearing Annie's laughter and lurching toward her, only to slap a bale of hay or the barn wall or one time the tabby cat that hissed and swiped at his arm. This sent the entire group into fits of laughter.

Finally, he caught the littlest nephew, a small tyke with white-blond hair and blue eyes. "I'm It? I'll never catch anyone."

"I'll help you…"

"His name is Teddy." Annie pulled the blindfold from Levi's hands and began to tie it around her nephew's eyes.

"Teddy?"

"Short for Theodore."

"I'll help you, Teddy."

"You will?" Teddy jerked his head in Levi's direction, though he couldn't see him as the blindfold was now firmly in place.

"Sure, just follow my voice and ignore everyone else."

It only took a couple of minutes.

Teddy's older *schweschder* Molly happened to trip and fall in the hay. Lucky for Teddy. He fell on her claiming, "I got ya. You're It. We did it, Levi."

They played another half hour, Teddy sticking close to Levi the entire time. When the children finally decided they were hungry again and ran from the barn, Levi collapsed on top of a bale of hay.

"Young ones wear you out."

"Oh, you're worn out, are you?"

"*Ya.* Aren't you?"

"I suppose." She glanced out the door and then back at him as if she was uncertain whether she should stay. As if she didn't know whether she should chance being alone with him.

"You can sit down, Annie. I won't bite."

"I never said you would."

"Then why does it feel like you've been avoiding me all day?"

"Avoiding you? Why would I do that?"

"I don't know. That's why I brought it up."

She rolled her eyes but sat down on an overturned crate.

"We should talk about our first date."

"We should call it something else."

"Really? Like what?"

"I don't know." She swiped at a lock of hair that had fallen free of her *kapp*. "Doesn't matter, I guess."

"I thought the point was we want your parents to think we're dating."

"Yes, yes…"

"And then it won't work, and then they'll leave you alone." He smiled triumphantly. "See? I was listening."

"Fine. So where are you taking me on this date? I was thinking a fancy restaurant…"

"What?"

"Or maybe even an *Englisch* movie. I love the popcorn and soda there."

"Do you know how much those cost?" He realized too late that she was baiting him. Feeling ridiculous, he countered with, "This whole dating thing—where it's assumed the guy will pay for everything—is not fair."

"Oooh. Are you thinking of bucking tradition? Notice I use the word *buck*. I'm trying to make you feel comfortable with some Texas slang."

This was the Annie he liked. The one who teased him with a smile that said, *Come on, walk into this trap.*

"I rode a bucking bronco once."

"You don't say?"

"Cracked two ribs when he threw me."

"So you learned your lesson?"

"What lesson would that be?"

"To stay off bucking broncos."

"*Nein.* See, bronco riding is a sport in Texas. They really enjoy it—like we do baseball."

"People don't crack their ribs in baseball."

"Well, normally they don't, but they could. That's not the point." He started to explain rodeo competitions to her, but she held up a hand and stopped him.

"You can bore me with this on our date. Where are we going?"

Suddenly he knew where he wanted to take her. "Let's go snag some of those leftover oatmeal raisin bars."

"We just ate."

"Hours ago. I'm starving."

"Spoken like a man."

"Women don't get hungry? Come on. You barely ate anything at lunch."

Annie had stood and was brushing hay off her dress. She stopped, her hand halfway down her apron, her eyes squinting and a line forming between her brows. "You were watching me eat?"

"I was trying to find time to talk to you."

"And so you followed me out here?"

"I'm not a stalker. We needed to plan our not-date. So what about it?"

"What about what?"

"Those oatmeal bars."

"They're bound to be gone already...the kids had a fifteen-minute start on us." A mischievous smile teased at her lips—very pretty pink lips, he suddenly noticed. "I might know where some are put back in the kitchen."

"You don't say."

"I could be persuaded to show you."

Levi stepped closer, reached out and plucked

a piece of hay from her *kapp*. She stood frozen, like a deer caught midstride.

"I'd like that." His voice suddenly sounded husky and low, sounded like a person he didn't recognize. He moved closer, wondering if he had the courage to kiss her. But either he was reading the mood wrong or Annie was not having any of it. She thrust the red dishcloth in his hands and said, "Stay close. If the *kinner* see what we're up to, we'll starve. We're outnumbered and don't stand a chance."

But Levi's thoughts were no longer focused on snacks or games of tag or even bull riding. He was thinking of one thing, and at the moment she was wearing a pretty dark blue dress and leading him across a rain-soaked yard.

Chapter Eight

Tuesday afternoon Annie waited on her front porch for Levi to arrive.

"Where is he taking you?" Her *mamm* was working on yet another baby blanket. They seemed to sprout from her knitting needles. This one was in pink, white and lavender.

"I don't know. He wouldn't say."

"It's so nice to see you getting out and having some fun. You work entirely too much, in my opinion."

Annie didn't answer that. She was already regretting this plan of theirs. She should be spending the afternoon sketching out ideas for the Hoschstetler wedding, though in truth she had two more weeks to get ready for that, and it was a small gathering—only a hundred and fifty guests.

"That sweater looks very nice on you."

"You made it for me."

"I remember, but you hardly ever wear it."

Annie fingered the light wool. It was a pretty burgundy and always reminded her of fall. It was true she rarely wore it, as she seldom did anything social and it was too nice for everyday clothes. Why had she even picked it for today? It wasn't like she needed to dress up for Levi Lapp.

As if thinking his name had the power to make him appear, Levi pulled into their lane.

How he'd managed to get off work early on a Tuesday, she had no idea. But he'd insisted that two in the afternoon was the best time so she'd agreed. What else could she do?

Annie tried not to blush as her *mamm* reminded them there was no need to hurry home. Before she could back out of the date, they were in the buggy traveling down the lane.

"How was your day?" Levi asked.

No doubt he was merely being polite, but she found herself telling him about the upcoming wedding and how Rachel Hoschstetler was having a small group.

"One hundred and fifty? Doesn't sound small to me."

"You've been to plenty of Amish weddings. You know what I mean."

"I guess."

"If you have ten siblings and they have ten children."

"I can do the math…"

"So you see what I mean, plus there's all the *aentis* and *onkels*. But Rachel, her family is small on her *mamm*'s side. She was an only child."

"I'm surprised they hired you if the gathering is so small."

She glared at him. Now, this was the Levi she expected, not the play-it-nice guy who wanted to know how her day had been, but the snarky one who questioned her ability to run a business.

"Why are you looking at me that way? My hat crooked?"

She didn't want to talk about his cowboy hat again. That was a ploy he often used to change the topic. She wasn't falling for it. "How could you say such a thing?"

"What did I say?"

"That you were surprised they would hire me."

"I am surprised." As if hearing what he was saying for the first time, he began to stammer, "Um…that's not what I meant."

"Oh, it isn't?"

"*Nein.* What I meant was…well, I was just wondering out loud why Amish who seldom eat out and never hire someone to help with the housework would hire someone to cook for a wedding. But now that I think about it, I guess you explained it to me that first night."

"You were actually listening?"

"Amish families hire you because a wedding is a tremendous amount of work. In fact, it's almost impossible for one family to do the work to prepare for a large wedding. But if this Rachel only has a small family, then I'm surprised they'd hire you."

He smiled in her direction, as if he'd cleared it all up.

Which he had, sort of. She was definitely too quick to jump to the wrong conclusion with Levi.

"Okay. Now I see what you mean."

"Gut."

"Her *mamm* is sick. She has MS and some days are harder than others. So her *dat* offered to hire me."

"Now that makes sense."

Annie had been so caught up in their conversation that she hadn't paid any attention to where he was driving. They'd traveled through Goshen and popped out the other side. They passed the Dairy Queen and the Best Western, and then Levi pulled off the main road.

"Fidler Pond?"

"Ya. Have you been here before?"

"Nein. I've wanted to but haven't found the time."

"I thought a few hours away from the farm might be nice."

"Huh."

"And I haven't tried my hand at a paddleboat in quite some time."

"They have paddleboats?" She felt an uncharacteristic surge of excitement. She loved paddling around in the water. Had she told him that? How could he have known?

Levi was parking the buggy, careful to pick a shady spot in an area that wasn't paved over. "Don't want Petunia standing on concrete for hours."

They were going to spend hours together?

Before she could dwell on that terrifying thought, he'd tugged on her hand and pulled her toward the small rental shack. As he started to pay, she remembered his lecture about men being expected to pay for everything on a date, about how unfair it was. She hadn't thought about that much. Then again, she hadn't been on very many dates.

"I can pay half." She opened her purse to fetch some money.

"I've got this." When she started to protest, he added, "We'll do dinner Dutch and you can pay for dessert."

"You expect this date to last that long?"

"Hope springs eternal…"

His tone had turned suddenly serious, and she found she couldn't quite meet his gaze. Why was Levi always surprising her? Teasing one minute and looking at her with those blue eyes she could drown in the next.

Instead of dwelling on it, she tossed her head and said, "Fine, but I get to pick the color of the boat."

She chose the bright yellow one, and before she could stop to think about how close they were going to be forced to sit, they were out in the middle of the small pond, laughing at the fish and splashing one another with the water.

After an hour of paddling, which was more strenuous exercise than she remembered, Levi dropped her off near some shade trees and returned to the paddleboat shack for the deposit he'd paid. She shouldn't have been surprised, but she was when he came walking down the trail carrying two cold sodas, two fishing poles and a small box of worms.

"Really? You bought worms?" It sounded critical even to her ears, so she bumped her shoulder against his and said, "Big Tom would have been happy to dig some up for us."

"*Gut* point." He popped the soda and handed it to her, then opened his own and drank down half of it. "But Big Tom isn't here, and I want to know if you can fish."

"Of course I can fish."

"Bet you don't know how to put a worm on a hook."

"Seriously?"

"Show me."

When she'd done so, he wiggled his eyebrows and said, "Little Annie is full of surprises. Now do mine. I can't stand to touch the things."

She couldn't help laughing at his expression of disgust as she threaded another worm on his hook. A guy who didn't like baiting a hook? Maybe in Texas they did it differently. Maybe there the fish jumped out of the water and into the boat with a little coaxing.

They caught a dozen perch in the next hour, then returned their poles and gave the remainder of their worms to a pair of *Englisch* boys. They looked to be under ten years old and had cane poles but only a couple of worms in a tin can.

"Thanks," the boys exclaimed, dashing off toward the water.

As they were walking back toward the buggy, Levi bumped her shoulder and asked, "Ready for some dinner?"

"You don't have to do that, Levi."

"I don't have to take you to dinner? So you think I'd take you home hungry?"

"I think I know your opinion on the terrible cost of dating."

"*Ya*, for sure and certain it's expensive. I paid two bucks for those worms." Waiting to be sure that she knew he was kidding, he added, "Your parents would never believe this was a real date if I took you home without feeding you."

They ate at the Dairy Queen, which had the added benefit of buggy parking. Sitting in the booth, watching Petunia munch on fall grass, Annie marveled at the odd twists and turns her life seemed to take. A month ago, she hadn't even known Levi Lapp. Now she was on a pretend date with him. Would wonders never cease?

"That's one thing they don't have in Texas." Levi wadded his wrapper into a ball and tossed it on top of the tray.

"Say that again."

"That's one thing they don't have in Texas—designated buggy parking."

Annie pulled on first one ear and then the other. "You must have splashed water in my ears when we were on that paddleboat. I thought you just said there's something Texas doesn't have."

"Go ahead. Make fun of me, but it's true. They don't have everything."

"They don't have Dairy Queens?"

"Of course they do. Actually, Texas has more DQs than any other state."

"You're making that up."

"*Nein*, I'm not."

His mind was like a buggy wheel stuck in a rut. Everything he saw, thought or heard he twisted into something about Texas. He was incorrigible.

"Tell me three things you don't like about Texas."

"Let's get dessert first."

They'd both had a burger and shared fries at a table inside. Levi bussed the table while Annie stood staring at the ice cream options. When he pulled out his wallet to pay, she stopped him.

"No way. You paid for dinner. I'm buying dessert. I intend to pay my way in this relationship."

Levi shrugged and ordered a large sundae. She settled for a dipped cone.

They took the ice cream outside and sat at one of the picnic tables, watching the *Englischers* and Amish come and go.

"That's one thing I enjoy about Goshen that I'd sort of forgotten." He pointed at a buggy, waiting in the drive-in behind a pickup truck.

"I'm not following."

"The two parts of the community have become used to one another here. Sure we have the occasional tourist trying to snap pictures…"

"Happens every time I come to town."

"And some *Englischers* still complain that Amish are willing to work for too low a wage."

"There was an article in the paper on that this week."

"But overall, it seems the Amish here have figured out how to remain separate while they also work seamlessly with the *Englisch*."

"I don't know if it's seamless." Annie paused to lick at a bit of ice cream that was running down her cone. "It's true though that we do work well together. Employers understand that we don't work on Sundays. And Amish understand that *Englischers* are simply trying to run a profitable business, which is important if we want the jobs."

"It's a *gut* situation for both groups. It's what I hope and pray we can have in our new community."

"Uh-uh. You don't get to jump into daydreaming. Now tell me three things that you don't like about this great state of yours."

Annie thought he'd brush her off, that he'd claim he needed to get back to Old Simon. She honestly wasn't sure he could do it. Look at his dream realistically? Was that even possible? Or did it stop being a dream at that point? But instead of changing the subject or claiming he needed to leave, Levi seemed to be thoughtfully considering her question.

Levi was surprised to find he was enjoying the pretend date with Annie. He'd grown used to her skepticism about Texas, so it no longer irritated him as it once had. Unlike when he'd first met her, he no longer took it personally. It helped that he understood her reasons for wanting to stay in Indiana.

"What you're asking, it's hard to do," he admitted.

"Hard? Why is it hard? Every person, every place has negative qualities."

"It's kind of like your grandparents."

"My grandparents?"

"Do you remember them?"

"Of course."

"So tell me about them."

"Dat's parents were quite a bit older, so they passed when I was young. Mamm's parents, they lived down the road. It hasn't been that long since Mammi and Daddi passed. I grew up as much at their house as I did at my own. I used to go there after school sometimes instead of going home. I'd help Mammi with her garden or work on a quilt with her."

"Tell me three things you didn't like about your *mammi*."

"I loved my *mammi*."

"Of course you did, but every person, every place has negative qualities."

She ducked her head and gave him a look when he quoted her words back to her. But he knew Annie well enough to know she wouldn't back away from a challenge.

"Okay. I see what you're doing. It is hard to remember the negative, or maybe we just choose not to remember." She stood up, walked to a trash barrel and tossed her napkin into it. When she came back to the picnic table, she was smiling. "Mammi was a sweetheart. I loved her dearly, but she wasn't perfect. She always wore this smelly lotion that she was certain helped with her arthritis. I remember being embarrassed at church thinking everyone else must be able to smell it, that surely she could go one day without putting it on."

"Probably other people wore it too."

"Oh, they did. In fact, they still do. When I catch a whiff of the stuff now, it always brings back *gut* memories of sitting by her side."

"But don't you see? Time changes the way we think of something. We tend to remember all the positive aspects or all the negative aspects. We don't have a very balanced view of things in our past."

"We see the past with rose-colored glasses."

Was that what he'd done for the last twelve years? If so, he needed to stop right now. He was convincing other families to risk a lot in order to move with him. How could he do that if he wasn't willing to look at what they were doing objectively?

"I was only fourteen when we left Texas. By

that time, my *dat* was sick. He had prostate cancer, though he wasn't diagnosed until we'd been back in Goshen for six months."

"I'm so sorry, Levi. I didn't know."

"I was a rambunctious teenager who was happy where he was. I had friends in Texas, and I had Tate Calloway—"

"Who was that?"

Levi sighed. He hadn't allowed himself to think about Tate in a long time. When he did, the pain still felt fresh. The man had been like family to him, and he hadn't even been able to attend his funeral. "He was our neighbor. He was a *gut* man."

"Sounds as if he was more than a neighbor."

"*Ya.* My *dat*…he had a hard time farming in Texas. It was nearly impossible to do so successfully, especially then. The bishop allowed us to try…not modern technology exactly but some irrigation techniques that helped. But Dat was stubborn and insisted on doing things the old way, and the old ways didn't work in the Texas dirt, especially during a drought."

The sky was growing dark, and Levi realized that the dinner crowd was thinning out at the Dairy Queen, but he wasn't ready to leave. The October evening was a perfect temperature, and Annie seemed like a different person tonight. She almost seemed to be enjoying her time with him.

As goofy as it sounded—even in his own head—
he didn't want the night to end. So instead of suggesting they drive home, he leaned back against
the picnic table and found a comfortable position.

"Tate was your stereotypical Texan. He had
calloused hands, a farmer's tan, and a slow way
of talking. He worked hard and was faithful to his
friends and family. I guess he became like a father to me. We didn't have any other family there,
and the farms were spread out a bit which made
it difficult to see one another during the week."

"There's one negative thing."

"*Ya*, I guess it was. It was probably natural to
become close to any neighbor within shouting
distance—even if he was a crusty old *Englisch*
cowboy."

"He became like an *onkel* to you?"

"I guess he did." He glanced at Annie, surprised that she had understood the situation so
quickly. He barely understood it himself. "Tate
taught me how to ride a horse proper-like. He
gave me my first Stetson. He even paid my entrance fee in the rodeo."

"And your parents were okay with that?"

Levi shrugged. He couldn't really remember
his parents' response. "They didn't seem to notice what I was doing then. I guess they were too
busy trying to pull a living out of the Texas dirt."

"A second negative thing."

He would have taken offense, but Annie didn't sound gleeful about pointing out the undesirable aspects of Texas. She looked completely caught up in his story.

"I guess. Anyway, my point is that those years were the best time in my life, so I remember the positive, like you do with your *mammi*."

"What happened then? Why did the community dissolve?"

"Drought, I think, and *ya*, that would be a third thing that's not so great about Texas. Here in Indiana, if it doesn't rain for a week we think we're having a drought. In Texas, it can go months with no rain, and then it comes all at once, flooding everything in sight."

"You really know how to sell a place." Her words didn't surprise him, but when she reached out and squeezed his hand, he almost jumped out of his suspenders.

"Don't worry, Levi. I'm not flirting with you." She smiled at him as if he'd just offered her a new pony. "But I understand now that those years in Texas were special to you. How long did you stay here in Goshen? Because I don't remember..."

"You were still a *youngie* then, and we would have been at different schoolhouses."

"I should be able to remember something of your being here if it was only twelve years ago."

"Twelve years is a long time." The calendar

in his head never forgot that date. He'd been trying to get back to Texas since the day they'd left. "You were probably still in school."

"*Ya.* I was."

"We came back here, and before we could really settle in, Dat was diagnosed. Prostate cancer usually moves slowly, but the kind Dat had moved fast. I can see now that was probably a blessing. At least he wasn't in pain for a long time."

He stood and nodded toward the buggy. They walked close together across the parking area. It felt strangely intimate, as if they were on a real date, as if he should reach out and take her hand. "He died three months after his diagnosis. Those were…they were tough months."

"I can't even imagine."

"My *mamm* was grieving, and my family was renting a place that was in pretty bad shape. Then my *mamm* met my stepfather—he was visiting his family here in Goshen one Sunday. Next thing I knew, we were packing up and moving to Pennsylvania."

He checked the horse, then helped Annie up into the buggy. Once they were on the road, he glanced at her, a little embarrassed that he had shared so much.

If it bothered her, he couldn't tell.

Their ride home was a quiet one, but it was a

comfortable silence. He didn't feel the need to jump in and talk about horses or boots or crops.

When he pulled down her lane, she said, "My life, I guess it's been pretty easy compared to yours."

"Every life has its burdens."

"Maybe, but you've been through a lot for someone so young. It's no wonder that you want to go back to a time, to a place, where you were happy."

"So you'll help me?"

"Nein."

He could feel more than see her smile as he pulled the horse to a stop in front of her house.

"But maybe I'll stop fighting you so hard."

She hopped out of the buggy. He leaned over before she could close the door. "Don't you think you should stay here a few minutes? Maybe we should kiss a little so your parents will believe this is a real date."

Her laughter was soft and sweet, and instead of it hurting his feelings, he found himself whistling as he turned the mare toward Simon's. He probably wasn't any closer to his dream, but something had happened tonight. He'd found a friend, and that didn't happen every day. Friendship, he'd learned over the years, was a precious thing. He could pause in his quest long enough to appreciate that *Gotte* had put Annie Kauffmann directly in his path.

The only question was, what was he supposed to do now?

Chapter Nine

Annie's plan was working, perhaps a little too well.

"You two were out late last night."

"I was home by dark, Mamm."

"Nearly."

"Okay, it was a few minutes after dark."

"I guess you had a *gut* time."

Annie stared over the rim of her coffee cup at her mother. Perhaps if she drank down the entire thing before answering, she'd find the patience to keep up this little charade of being romantically interested in Levi.

Then she remembered about his *dat*, dying when Levi was only a *youngie*.

She remembered telling him about her *mammi*, and how much she missed the dear woman.

She sipped her coffee, offered up a prayer of

gratitude that she still had her parents around to meddle in her affairs and smiled at her *mamm*.

"We went to Fidler Pond, walked a little, fished a little…"

"You fished?"

"I even baited Levi's hook for him. Turns out, he's a bit squeamish."

Which started them both laughing and suddenly her irritation melted away. Later, as she was setting the table for breakfast, Annie realized that part of her bad mood was her own fault. She didn't like deceiving her parents. She should just tell them that she wasn't interested in Levi as anything but a *freind*.

But then they'd point out what a fine young man he was.

They'd bring up that she wasn't getting any younger.

They would insist that there was no hurry, but really how many chances did she expect to have? *Nein*. She wasn't going through that conversation again. Better to pretend to like Levi in a romantic way, then after a few dates she could explain that they simply weren't compatible.

It was a deception, and she felt guilty about that.

But it was the easiest path for everyone.

Levi didn't eat breakfast with them, claiming he'd eaten at Old Simon's. She couldn't imagine what type of food that might have been, but she shrugged as if it didn't bother her and handed him a mug of coffee.

"Mind if I carry this to the barn?"

"Suit yourself."

He'd been avoiding eye contact, but now he looked at her, smiled and touched the brim of his cowboy hat.

That hat.

She'd closed her eyes and was thinking of how to get it away from him, how to casually replace it with a proper Amish hat, when he turned and walked away. After breakfast, she saw Levi and her *dat* head out to the south pasture. Probably planting the winter crop. If her *dat* had talked about his plans for that day during breakfast, she hadn't been paying attention.

Not that it mattered to her what Levi Lapp did all day.

She went out to the garden to harvest the last of their vegetables. A half hour later, she was digging up the last of the potatoes when her sister Nicole called out to her.

"I didn't hear your buggy pull up."

"We walked."

"You're a brave woman venturing out alone across the pasture with that group."

She looked up into the kitchen window and saw Nicole's three children sitting at the table.

No doubt they were being treated to cold milk and a good-sized peanut butter cookie by Annie's *mamm*.

"They were full of energy this morning," Nicole explained. "I decided a walk would tire them out..."

"I hope you used the stroller."

"I did. Anyway, I was hoping the time away would help everyone take a nap this afternoon."

"How are you feeling?"

"Gut." Nicole placed a hand on top of her stomach as she sat down in the dirt next to Annie. "This is the *gut* part, before my ankles start to swell and I have constant indigestion from the baby taking up the space where my stomach is supposed to be."

"You make it sound lovely."

Nicole picked up a handful of dirt and sifted it through her fingers. "It's better than that—I think it may be the most amazing thing a woman can experience."

Annie didn't bother answering. She'd seen her *schweschder* in this phase before—two times before. She'd also seen her when she could barely waddle down the steps, and when she'd been carrying the twins she'd looked positively huge. Pregnancy wasn't a picnic in the park, but for now Nicole was enjoying her condition so why argue with her?

"Heard you went out with Levi last night."

"Oh, good grief."

"What? It's not like anyone was gossiping."

"Right. So a little bird must have told you, *ya*?"

"Beth saw Levi turn into the park when she was coming home from work. Martha saw you at the Dairy Queen as she was leaving. Guess you didn't notice either one of them."

"Guess I didn't."

"She said you only had eyes for Levi."

"Oh, come on. Does that even sound like me?"

"It doesn't, which is why I'm sitting here asking you questions."

Annie pushed her shovel under a particularly stubborn potato and pulled from the top. She was rewarded with a spray of dirt. Seeing her covered in dirt, Nicole began to giggle. Annie wanted to be offended, but she couldn't pull it off. Before she knew it, she was laughing along with her. It felt *gut* to relax with her *schweschder*, and she knew deep in her heart that it would feel even better if she were to confess the truth to her.

"I'm going to tell you something, but promise to keep it to yourself."

Nicole nodded. "I promise."

So she told her about the harvest, how her parents had begun giving her *the look* and whispering when they thought she couldn't hear, how she'd come up with a plan to pretend to date Levi.

"And they fell for it?"

"Well, *ya*, because they already think we're falling for each other. People see what they want to see."

"How long do you expect to keep this up?"

"I don't know—three or four dates, I guess. That's about the longest any relationship I've ever had has lasted."

"And you can't just tell them that you're not interested?"

"You know I've tried that before. They don't listen."

"It's because they worry about you. We all do."

"Why? Because I have a successful business and I'm a happy, single Amish woman?"

"Don't twist your bonnet strings into a knot. I'm just saying that we care about you, and we want to see you happily settled."

"I'm only twenty-four. It's not like I'm ancient."

"And no one is suggesting that you are."

Annie stood, brushed the dirt from the back of her dress, then reached down and helped Nicole to her feet. She thrust the basket of vegetables into her *schweschder*'s hands and picked up her gardening tools. They walked toward the back porch in silence, but before they climbed the steps, Nicole stayed her with the touch of her hand.

"Just be careful."

"How do you mean?"

"With your heart. Beth and Martha both said that you looked happy, and when you talk about Levi, your eyes light up."

"You've been reading too many romance books again. Eyes don't actually light up."

"It's just… I don't want to see Levi break your heart."

"You think I'll have a broken heart? I thought you liked Levi."

"Sure, I do, but everyone knows how you feel about moving to Texas."

"I can't believe you're even considering it."

Nicole didn't address that. She was apparently bound and determined to issue her warning. "It doesn't seem likely that Levi will change his mind and stay here in Goshen."

"And I wouldn't want him to. It's obvious Texas is where he belongs." Which sounded so strange coming out of her mouth that she almost pinched herself to see if she was awake or in some bizarre dream.

As she followed Nicole into the house, she realized that it was true. Levi did belong in Texas. That much was obvious from their long talk the evening before. Which left her in quite an awkward position—finding a way to stymie his plans or at least remove her family from the details at the same time that she was hoping and praying he would be able to move forward.

Levi didn't see much of Annie on Wednesday, and was surprised when she wasn't at the breakfast table on Friday morning. If he were honest with himself, he would admit that he had been avoiding her on Wednesday. He'd even skipped breakfast so he wouldn't have to sit and make idle chatter. For some reason he wasn't sure he could do that, not after they'd shared so much with each other on their first date.

He'd agreed to work for her *dat*, and he'd agreed to this pretend dating plan, but he'd expected to be able to keep himself aloof from it all. It wasn't working. He could feel his wall of disinterest caving. He could feel himself becoming distracted.

The less time he spent around her, the better. Then again, they were supposed to be stepping out together.

So as he accepted the mug of strong coffee and sat down at the table, he caved in to his curiosity and asked her parents where she'd gone so early in the day.

"She's helping Priscilla prepare for a wedding they are catering tomorrow."

"Another Saturday wedding?"

"*Ya.* I remember when most weddings were

on Tuesdays and Thursdays, but we've grown so much that Saturday weddings are becoming a common occurrence."

"Oh."

"Would you like me to give Annie a message?"

"I didn't realize she would be working, though everyone knows that October is the marrying season around here. I should have thought of that."

"What were you going to ask her?" Alton reached for the platter of bacon and put four pieces on his plate.

"I thought she might want to go to town with me tomorrow night. You know, since we're stepping out and all."

Annie's parents shared a look, and Levi wanted to hide under the kitchen table. Why had he even brought it up? Now they were looking at him as if he'd invented the hay baler.

He thought they might give him the standard talk of always being respectful to their daughter.

Or maybe they'd bring up what a fine *fraa* she would make, as if he couldn't see that with his own two eyes.

Instead, Lily scooped another helping of eggs onto his plate, and Alton started talking about the fence work they needed to do that day.

When he was leaving to follow Alton to the barn, Lily pulled him aside. "Annie's wedding tomorrow is an early one, and they're only having the noonday meal, not the evening."

"Ya?"

"I suspect she'd enjoy some time out after that. You could leave her a note, and I'll give it to her."

"Danki, I'll do that."

He borrowed paper and a pen and worked on the message at lunch, eating his sandwich out at the picnic table. He ruined three good sheets of paper before he settled on what to say. Reading back over it, he wondered how he'd ever had a date in his life. He certainly wasn't very good at this.

Annie,
I know you're working tomorrow morning. Would you like to go out for pizza tomorrow night? The fall festival is happening in town and we could walk through the booths, listen to the bands, stuff like that. If you want. If you don't, I understand. In fact, you probably don't, so you can just ignore this letter. But on the off chance you do want to, leave me a message at the phone shack. I'll check it around noon.
Yours,
Levi

Yours?
What did that even mean?

Why did people sign letters that way?

And under that was a deeper worry. Was her mother going to read it before giving it to her? Should he have added a heart or said something about kissing her so they'd believe that something romantic was going on?

"We're not *youngies*," he muttered to himself, folding the letter and sticking it into his pocket. He'd hand it to Lily before leaving. Annie had said they needed to go on three dates, and if it helped her out, then he'd do it. Though this letter-writing thing was nothing short of humiliating.

The afternoon passed more slowly than seemed possible. He kept checking his watch to see if it was time to go. Finally, he finished the last of the chores Alton had asked him to do and bounded up the steps and into the kitchen. On Fridays, Lily always had his pay for the week ready for him, and he'd need that if he was going to take Annie to the festival. The wages he'd earned the previous weeks were already in the bank, in what he thought of as his Moving-to-Texas account, and he didn't want to use any money from it. Folks thought that Amish didn't use banks, but it wasn't like he could keep money under his mattress. Well, he could, but it would be a silly thing to do.

So he needed his week's pay if he was going to take Annie out the next day. Not that he expected her to say yes, but better to be prepared than not.

Lily had wrapped up some of the dinner she was cooking. She handed it to Levi. Apparently, everyone thought that he and Old Simon were starving. It was true that both of them were growing tired of egg sandwiches, but they certainly weren't going hungry.

Levi stared down at the basket full of freshly fried chicken, baked potatoes and some sort of dessert. He should feel hungry, but instead his stomach felt as if he were coming down with a bug.

"I'll give her the note," Lily assured him.

"Danki." He turned to go, but turned back around when Lily called his name.

"We appreciate your help around here. You've been a real blessing to us."

He nodded, his throat suddenly feeling as if he were choking on something. Had his own family ever said those words to him? He didn't think so. He thought they were probably glad he'd left. So why did it seem that Annie's family was always so glad to have him around? And why was he letting himself get closer to them when for sure and certain he'd be gone in six months?

Levi was completely surprised when he checked the phone booth on Saturday afternoon and he had a short message from Annie. She must be more eager to get their three dates over with than he thought.

When he arrived at her house, she was dressed in a freshly laundered dark orange dress with a white apron. She looked as pretty as the fall leaves dancing across the porch.

"You're sure you feel like doing this?"

"After today's wedding? *Ya.* I'm sure."

She proceeded to tell him of the squirrels stealing the nuts on the tables, a bridesmaid who broke out in hives and a young nephew who decided that putting his finger in each of the wedding cupcakes was a fun idea.

He was laughing so hard by the time they reached downtown Goshen that he'd forgotten all about being nervous. Had he been nervous? Maybe he'd built this up to be more than it was. They were becoming *freinden*, and that was *gut*. The fact that they were pretending to be something else, that wasn't great but he thought he could live with it.

He actually relaxed and started having a good time.

That is, until they ran into the newlyweds Avery and Beth.

"We'd heard you two were stepping out."

Beth clasped Avery's hand as if she were afraid to walk through the fall festival alone. Or maybe that was what love looked like. Levi wasn't sure.

"*Ya*. We're dating for sure and certain." Levi ran a thumb under his right suspender. "I'm looking for a missus to take to Texas, so it seemed a smart thing to do."

Annie's elbow in his ribs caught him by surprise.

"Not that I'm thinking of moving to Texas," she corrected. "But anyway, let's not talk about us. How are you two?"

The next twenty minutes they spent walking through the fall booths, listening to Avery describe his new mare, new buggy and new home. Had these two waited a long time to marry or were they simply fortunate enough to be given everything a young couple could possibly want? Levi was so irritated he could barely concentrate on what everyone was saying.

Plus, his mind was distracted by Annie.

She was standing shoulder to shoulder with him. He wasn't used to being in such close proximity to a beautiful woman.

And she'd been holding his hand since they'd run into Beth and Avery. He wasn't great at holding hands—not that he had a lot of experience with it. He never knew if you should lace your fingers together or simply clasp each other's hand. And what happened when your hands started sweating like his were now? Should he pull his hand away and wipe it on his pants? Or pretend he didn't notice?

On top of those questions, he kept worrying he was squeezing her hand too hard.

Why did everything feel so awkward?

He even tripped twice over absolutely nothing.

Finally, Beth and Avery hurried off to ride the merry-go-round together, which sounded ridiculous to Levi. Weren't the rides for *kinner*? Why would an adult ride one? Slapping his hat against his leg, he voiced his irritation with the two.

"They're all right. They're just in *lieb*." Annie looked down at her hand clasping his, dropped it like a hot potato and muttered, "Sorry about that. Just trying to look authentic."

"They even have a new halter for the horse. If I heard of one more new thing, I think I might have had to do something desperate."

"Like?"

"I don't know…challenge him to an apple-bobbing contest, then reach over and push his head under? A good dunking in cold water might help him come to his senses."

Annie was smiling at him and shaking her head, so he kept going.

"Or I could suggest he get in the pie-throwing contest and then buy three pies to throw at him? Maybe I could have sent him into the corn maze and hoped he got lost for a few minutes. I was ready to pay for the merry-go-round just so they'd go."

"While you two were checking out the wood-craft booth, I had to listen to Beth talk about her new dishes, new bedding and new furniture."

"Were they both born with a silver spoon in their mouths?"

"They're Amish, remember. Just on the upper end of the simple scale, and they are usually very nice about it. I guess they're rather caught up in being newlyweds."

"I guess. We'd never act like that, though. You and I wouldn't lose our common sense or our manners just because we decided to get hitched."

Annie stepped back and nearly tripped over a hay bale that was painted like a pumpkin. Levi reached out for her arm, steadied her and then dropped his hand when she assured him she was fine.

"This date is not turning out like I planned," he said.

"It's a pretend date. How did you expect it to turn out?"

But before he could answer that, they bumped into the bishop and his wife. Annie once again stepped close to his side, slipped her arm through his so that they were like links in a paper chain. He could smell the soap she'd used to shampoo her hair, some sort of flowery-smelling lotion and, if he wasn't mistaken, perhaps a touch of cocoa. When he asked her about it, she started laughing. That was one thing he really liked about Annie. She laughed easily.

"That would be from the chocolate cake I made for the wedding."

"Chocolate cake?"

"It was a spur-of-the-moment decision. I had to replace the ruined cupcakes and we had plenty of flour, sugar and cocoa on hand."

They'd stepped away from the bishop and were headed toward the food booths.

"What did you mean before?" she asked. "You said this date wasn't turning out like you expected."

"I didn't count on running into so many people we know."

"*Ya*, Goshen is still a small town."

"I know what will cheer me up." He snagged her hand and pulled her toward the food booth with the longest line. After they'd purchased a turkey leg, corn dog, large fries, funnel cake, hot chocolate and sweet iced tea, they found a seat at one of the picnic tables toward the back. She started to sit across from him, but he shook his head and pulled her over to his side—so they were both facing the band, not because he wanted to sit next to her.

"This is perfect." Levi finally felt like he could

talk at a normal volume. "We can hear the band but not be overpowered by it. Have you ever noticed how loud *Englischers* play their music?"

But Annie wasn't paying attention to the band on the stage. She was staring at the tray of food he'd plopped on the table. "Are you really going to eat all of that?"

"Of course not. I bought half of it for you."

"Which half?"

"You said you like turkey legs…"

"I do."

"So do I. You can have the first half and I'll take what's left."

"We're splitting a turkey leg?"

"I had to try a corn dog. Fall festivals require corn dogs."

"So you get half the turkey leg and all the corn dog."

"I'll save you the second half."

"I've never shared a meal this way."

"Have you ever shared a meal at all?"

"Well, I had *bruders* growing up. They'd sometimes steal food from my plate when we were out in public."

"They did not."

"*Ya*, they did. Nathan was the worst about that. He'd always claim I wasn't going to finish it anyway."

"I like hearing about your family."

"You do?" She carefully chose a fry and put it into her mouth.

"Sure. They sound so…happy."

"Was your family not happy?"

"I don't know. I always thought the tension was normal, but maybe it wasn't. Maybe it was just that times were tough while we were in Texas, and then Dat getting sick and all as soon as we moved back here." He bit into the corn dog and groaned. "You have to try this."

Annie squirreled up her nose.

"What? Afraid of my germs?"

"Of course not."

He leaned toward her and lowered his voice. "If we were kissing…"

She scooted away as if he had chicken pox and she was afraid of catching it. "I think you must be really hungry because you're acting a little crazy."

"I am?" Levi could feel the smile growing on his face. He liked teasing Annie. He especially liked it when she blushed and seemed flustered. He slipped across the bench, pulling the tray of food with him. "We should sit closer. So we look authentic."

Instead of answering, she accepted the corn dog he was still offering her and took a big bite. "That is *gut*," she said with her mouth still full.

And then they were both laughing, and Levi

thought the night was turning out all right, maybe even better than he had imagined.

They finished their meal, took a stroll through the corn maze and watched children having their faces painted. They ran into a few more people they knew, and each time Annie stepped closer and reached for his hand. The last time, she didn't let go, so maybe she was trying to be prepared.

Or maybe...

Before he could finish that thought, he noticed Bishop Marcus hurrying toward them across the parking area.

"Levi, I've been looking all over for you."

"Why?"

"It's Old Simon. He's in the hospital."

Chapter Ten

Annie sat in the waiting room of the Goshen Medical Center. It wasn't her first time there. Over the years, they'd visited the facility whenever someone in their congregation was ill. Now Amish folks from their church filled the waiting room, a testament to how many lives Old Simon had touched.

"Still no word from Levi?" Nicole asked.

"*Nein*, and I can't believe you're here. Shouldn't you be home resting?"

"I'm pregnant, not sick."

"But the kids…"

"Mamm was happy to stay with them. She wanted me to come and sit with you."

Annie resisted the urge to roll her eyes.

"Someone needed to bring you home if Levi decides to stay."

"This room is full of people from our church.

I think I could have found a ride home." The words came out snippier than she'd intended, so she bumped her *schweschder*'s shoulder and added, "But thanks for coming. I appreciate it."

She felt as if her emotions had been through a clothes wringer. She wasn't sure what she was feeling, and her mind kept returning to Levi.

To the look on his face when the bishop had first told them Old Simon was ill.

His profile as he drove the buggy toward the hospital.

The way he'd reached out for her hand as they'd hurried toward the emergency room entrance.

She'd sat with him for two hours as the waiting room had slowly filled with people from their congregation, everyone eager to hear an update on Old Simon's condition. The only thing anyone knew was that a neighbor had found him collapsed in the kitchen when they stopped by to deliver fresh eggs.

"He was fine when I left him," Levi had insisted when they'd first sat down onto two plastic chairs. He picked up a magazine from the table which he continually rolled and unrolled in a tube.

Annie was certain it would never be flat again, but she didn't have the heart to correct him. Perhaps it was one reason they put the magazines there, so people would have something to do with their nervous energy.

An hour later, one of the doctors called him back to Old Simon's room.

"I'm surprised they let him go in to visit." Nicole had brought her knitting bag and proceeded to work on a baby blanket—yellow with blue-and-pink flowers. "You know how strict they are about only allowing family to see a patient."

"Levi has been in contact with Old Simon's eldest son, even before he moved here. He wanted to make sure it was all right for him to do so. He didn't want anyone thinking he was taking advantage of Simon."

"I didn't realize that. It was thoughtful of him to reach out that way."

"As soon as we arrived here at the hospital, he called Jonah, who gave the doctors permission to speak with Levi."

They waited another thirty minutes, the clock creeping past midnight. Somewhere around one in the morning, Levi came out, spoke quietly to Bishop Marcus and then sat down next to Annie.

Marcus raised a hand to quiet everyone. "Levi has met with the doctors, spoken on the phone with Jonah, and he's visited with Old Simon. It would seem that Simon has suffered from a stroke."

Murmurs of "mercy" and "*Gotte* be with him"

and "we'll keep praying" wafted through the group. When they'd quieted down, the bishop continued.

"The stroke mainly affected his left side, so Simon is considered a fall risk at this point. The doctors will monitor him another forty-eight hours, then he'll be sent to the rehab facility here in Goshen where they can work on restoring his strength to his left side. He is able to speak, and he's thanked all of you for being here and asked you to go home."

Soft laughter echoed around the room. Slowly in ones and twos, people began standing and gathering their things. Several offered to give Annie a ride home, but she told them she'd wait and go with Levi.

Nicole pulled her into a tight hug and said, "Remember what we talked about—guard your heart."

Soon the only three who remained were Levi, Annie and Bishop Marcus.

No one spoke for a few minutes. Levi broke the silence, leaning forward with his elbows propped on his knees and his fingers interlaced. "I should have noticed. He's been more forgetful than usual. Said we should drive over to Stephenville one day. Another time he confused the Red River with the Mississippi River."

"No reason for you to suspect that it was anything more than a slight forgetfulness," Annie tried to reassure him.

"*Ya*, but I could have insisted he see a doctor."

"I've never known Old Simon to respond well to such suggestions." Bishop Marcus was sitting in the chairs across from them, but the room was small and it felt as if they were in someone's living room.

"I'm so relieved that he's going to be okay." Annie wanted to reach out and clasp Levi's hand, but she stopped herself when she realized that might not be appropriate. They weren't promised to one another. They weren't even really dating.

The bishop cleared his throat. "It sounds as if he is…for now."

Levi's head jerked up suddenly. "What do you mean for now?"

"I've seen this before, is all I'm saying. Strokes are caused by cardiovascular disease. The condition is actually a cluster of diseases. Events such as a stroke are often followed by heart problems that require surgery for stents or bypasses. That's on top of the danger that another stroke might occur or even that he could develop a blood clot."

"But the doctor said—"

"That they'll rehab him. Yes, of course, but what I want you to realize is that this isn't something that will go away. It's something Old Simon is going to have to deal with from now on. Ultimately it means that Jonah is going to have to make a decision about where his father should live."

"What you're saying is that he's not going to Texas."

"Do you think that would be a wise decision? If he were your *dat*, would you want him moving to a smaller community and tackling the difficult work of starting a new district?" Marcus studied Levi, but he didn't rush him. Instead, he sat back and waited, patiently.

Levi dropped his head between his hands, and it seemed to Annie that a giant burden had been placed on his shoulders. Instead of letting it defeat him, though, Levi sat up straighter, squared his shoulders and looked Marcus straight in the eye.

Annie realized in that moment that she could love Levi Lapp—if things were different, if she'd met him five years earlier or five years later, if he were looking to marry and settle in Goshen.

"Nein," Levi said. "I don't believe it would be wise for him to go to Texas. He needs to be here, near his *freinden*. Or with his son. But he doesn't need to try something so physically taxing as moving and starting a new community."

Marcus nodded in agreement.

"He was the reason I came here. I thought… I thought it would be possible to finally realize my dream if I had the help of someone like Simon backing me."

"What you're trying to do, it might still be possible, Levi. But the Bible never said that our path would be easy, and your path just became a little harder. Pray about what has happened as well as what lies ahead, read the scripture, look to the wisdom of family and *freinden*. You will know what it is that you should do next."

The bishop stood, stepped closer and reached out a hand which he placed gently on each of their shoulders. "*Gotte* guide you through this difficult time," he said softly, and then he was gone.

Twenty minutes later a nurse came out and told them that Simon had been given something to help him sleep. She suggested they go home and get some rest, then come back in the morning. When they stepped out into the night, Annie looked up at the stars and marveled that only a few hours had passed. It seemed as if they'd been in the hospital for days.

They rode in silence. The sway and rhythm of the buggy and the clip-clop of the horse calmed the emotions churning through Annie's heart. She found her thoughts drifting to how Levi seemed to have matured since she'd met him. He no longer rushed at top speed into something. He'd been able to admit that it wasn't the best thing for Old Simon to move, even though it would be a setback to his own plans. He'd held up admirably to the pressure of the evening.

She thought she detected a softening in his attitude.

Perhaps he was beginning to see that his happiness and future weren't dependent on an ill-advised move to Texas.

At the very moment that thought passed through her mind, Levi sat up straighter and pushed his hat down on his head.

"Something wrong?"

"Only that I realize what a fool I've been."

"Fool...what do you mean?"

"The last few hours I've been thinking this was the end of everything that I've worked for."

"You're not going to move?"

"But now I realize it's *Gotte* testing me, same as he tested Job, same as he tested Abraham."

"I'm not following the comparison."

"This." His hand waved to include the horse, the road, the cold October night. "Certainly it was unexpected that Old Simon would take ill—though perhaps I should have been prepared for it. You all call him Old Simon for a reason."

"Many people are old but don't have strokes."

If Levi heard her he gave no indication. It was almost as if he were speaking to himself, as if he were working out some puzzle and he needed to verbalize the solution.

"Simon's illness doesn't mean I'm supposed to give up. It means I'm supposed to stay the course."

"That's what you took away from what Bishop Marcus said?"

"He reminded me that the Bible never said that our path would be easy."

"*Ya*, but—"

"We're to run the race set before us."

"Once we're certain what that race is."

"Fight the good fight."

"I'm not sure that verse refers to chasing a childhood dream."

"*Gotte* has plans for me. Plans for a future."

"*Ya*, but Levi, are you absolutely certain that future is in Texas?"

He glanced at her, studied her a moment, then looked away.

"You don't believe in my dream, Annie?"

"I didn't say that."

"I thought we were becoming friends."

"Of course we are."

"Then as my path becomes more difficult, I would think you would encourage me, not question me."

She didn't answer immediately. In truth, her temper had claimed her tongue. How could he be so stubborn and bullheaded? But she didn't think now was the time to share that question.

"The old ones, their proverbs come back to us at times like this. I used to laugh at my *daddi* when he quoted them, but now I can see that he was wise and trying to raise me up to be a *gut* man."

"Your *daddi* told you to move to Texas?"

"One of his favorite sayings was *No dream comes true until you wake up and go to work.*" He shook his head as if he couldn't believe what he was hearing or thinking or seeing. "I've been walking around like a *youngie*, head up in the clouds, wishing things would go my way. Now I see that it's time that I wake up and go to work."

Annie couldn't believe what she was hearing. Just when she thought Levi was finally coming to his senses, finally growing up and abandoning this ridiculous plan, he was in fact doing the exact opposite.

"Are you forgetting that you need three ministers?"

"And now I have none." Instead of hanging his head in despair, Levi stretched the muscles in his neck. "It's going to be a challenge. I need to get busy writing letters, visiting communities that are adjacent to ours. I can see now that I've been…distracted."

He flicked a glance her way, and Annie felt her temper ignite like a firecracker on the Fourth of July.

"Oh really? I'm so sorry if I've *distracted* you."

"Not your fault. I let it happen."

"You're telling me that's what this has been—what I have been—is a mere distraction."

"You said yourself that you're not interested in marrying." He pulled on the reins, directing the mare to turn down the lane that led to her house.

"Oh, trust me. I'm not, and if I were, it wouldn't be with someone who still thinks like a *youngie* on his *rumspringa*."

"And the fact that you continue to see it that way is proof that we're not intended for each other."

"I'll agree with that."

"As far as your parents thinking I'm *gut* dating material—"

"I will have no trouble setting them straight in that regard." The buggy had barely come to a stop, but Annie needed out of it immediately. She opened the door and practically jumped out.

If Levi was surprised by her abrupt departure, he didn't say anything. He certainly didn't call out after her.

How could he be so stubborn? So willful? So illogical?

She couldn't resist one last jab. Leaning back into the buggy she said, "Don't forget you'll need twelve to fifteen families."

"I haven't forgotten."

"And all those answers to my questions. Bishop Marcus said to be ready when we meet this Friday."

"Oh, I'll be ready." Now there was a gleam in his eyes that she could see even in the dim light of the moon hanging above them.

"And so will I."

"I didn't think you'd give up trying to stop me, Annie." His voice softened, and for just a moment she was reminded of the Levi who had held her hand at the fall festival. "Do your best, but don't blame me for holding tightly to my dream."

"You can hold as tight as you want. It doesn't mean it's going to happen. It doesn't make it the right thing for our community." She was so angry that her heart was racing and she could barely spit out the words. She heard her *mamm*'s voice in her head, reminding her that a handful of patience was worth more than a bushel of brains. The problem was that she was out of patience, and Levi was determined to ignore his brain.

"I guess that's for Marcus to decide," he reminded her.

"*Ya.* I guess it is."

"Then I'll see you at the meeting Friday."

"I'll be there." She slammed the buggy door hard enough to startle poor Petunia, and she was tempted to stop and apologize to the horse. Her pride pushed her up the porch steps and into the house. As she heard Levi drive away, she felt a nearly overwhelming flood of various emotions—relief that the farce of their dating was over, disappointment that he couldn't see what was so painfully obvious to her, and a tiny bit of regret that she'd allowed an Amish cowboy to work his way into her heart.

Annie gave up on trying to sleep a few minutes before five the next morning. All she'd managed to do was toss, turn and twist her covers into a knot. By the time she dressed, made her bed, and took care of her morning toiletry, she'd moved from a random sort of resentment to a very pointed, particular anger.

Not that she would let it affect her day.

She wasn't going to waste another minute stewing over Levi Lapp. She made the coffee, squeezed fresh orange juice, put up the dishes that were in the drainer, fried bacon and potatoes and was cracking eggs into the skillet when her mother walked into the room, yawning and widening her eyes as if to try to make sense of what she was seeing.

"Something wrong, dear?"

"Nein."

"You're up rather early."

Annie looked around in surprise. The table was set. She'd made fresh cinnamon rolls. Juice was in a pitcher and glasses at each place. Steam was coming from the pots and pans on the stove. She didn't remember doing any of it.

Annie shrugged and said, "Thought I'd get an early start on the day is all."

"You do remember it's Sunday, right?"

"Sure, *ya*. But…we still need to eat."

"Indeed." Her *mamm* added cream to her coffee and shuffled over to the table, still trying to fully open her eyes.

"Did I wake you?"

"I woke when your *dat* went out to the barn, but usually I take my time to get in here. Usually no one else is awake."

"Sorry."

"If I didn't know better, I'd think our kitchen cabinets had done something to offend you."

"The cabinets?"

"You were…" Her *mamm* gulped down more coffee and waved at the cabinets. "You were slamming them."

"Oh. Sorry."

"You already said that."

"*Ya.* I know."

"What's wrong? Is it Old Simon?"

"*Nein.* His condition is stable."

"And the outlook?"

"Rehab, probably followed by reduced activity." She grabbed a spatula and attacked the potatoes with it. They were browning nicely, but she needed to do something with her hands.

"Why don't you come and sit down?"

"I can't. Breakfast will burn."

By the time her father returned to the house, she had so many breakfast dishes on the table that it resembled Thanksgiving dinner.

"Well, what's the special occasion?" he asked.

"Annie is a bit agitated this morning," her *mamm* murmured.

"I heard that," Annie said.

"I should hope so, dear."

She rolled her eyes, petitioned God for patience and then sat down at the table. She had to admit, it was a lot of food for just three people.

"Let's pray." Her *dat* bowed his head.

One thing that Annie both loved and hated about their Amish tradition was that they often prayed silently. If someone else was praying aloud, she could sometimes distance herself from the things troubling her soul. At the moment, her options were to shut her eyes and only pretend to pray or bare her heart before God. So she did just that—admitting her anger and her humiliation and her fear. She didn't like those things about herself. She didn't want fear and embarrassment to rule her emotions or actions, but she also didn't see a way around the emotions that threatened to consume her. She asked *Gotte* for guidance, for patience, for wisdom and for strength.

She might have stayed with her head bowed for a much longer time, but her *dat* cleared his voice and said, "*Danki* for this day you've given us to rest, to draw closer to you and to spend time with those you've given us to love and care for. Amen."

Her amen coincided with her *mamm*'s. Tears pricked Annie's eyes, and she stared down at her lap.

She heard her *mamm* and *dat* speaking to one another, the words passing over her like clouds scuttling by on a summer day.

"Haven't had potatoes for breakfast in ages."

"Plus she cooked ham and bacon."

"Might be too full for lunch."

"We'll have to pretend to be hungry so as not to hurt Nicole's feelings."

"'Course that is hours away, and I used a lot of energy taking care of the chores."

"You always do, dear."

Annie pushed back her chair and stood. "I'm… I'm not hungry. I think I'll go to my room for a few minutes."

As she fled the kitchen, she heard them lower their voices. She had no doubt they were talking about her, were worried, but she couldn't think about that right now. Instead of going to her room, she rushed outside, down the porch steps and out to the pasture.

Perhaps a few moments alone, appreciating an absolutely perfect October Sunday, would calm her turbulent emotions.

"So you're mad at him because he still wants to move to Texas?" Nicole kept her attention focused on her three children. They were all sitting under a maple tree that was resplendent with red, gold and brown leaves. At the moment, Nicole's oldest child, Rachel, was covering Micah and Mitchell with leaves. The twins were sitting up and staring at their big *schweschder* as if she were the most entertaining thing they'd ever seen. When she'd dump more leaves on them, they would giggle, slap the leaves with their open hands and call out, "More," one of the few words they knew.

"I'm mad because obviously everything I thought was happening, wasn't. He was stringing me along…"

"But it was your idea to pretend date."

"I know it was."

"And you've known from the first day you met him that his goal is to move to Texas."

"Yes, but…"

"But what?"

Annie avoided her sister's gaze. For as long as she could remember, Nicole had been able to read her every thought, every feeling, simply by looking at her. Maybe that was Nicole's gift—an ability to see into the hearts of people. The problem was that Annie wasn't sure she wanted her heart to be seen. She wasn't sure she had the courage to admit her dreams and heartbreak to herself. But she did know that she hated these feelings—this pent up anger and frustration and disappointment.

Finally, she raised her eyes to her sister. "My heart hurts." The words brought a fresh cascade of tears.

"Oh, honey."

Nicole scooted closer and pulled her into a hug, rubbing her back and giving her a few moments to compose herself.

Annie finally pulled away, swiped at the tears running down her face, and attempted a laugh. "You warned me."

"I did."

"This is why I cater weddings instead of trying to have one myself. It's too painful."

"Not always."

"I guess."

Rachel ran toward them, her arms filled with leaves. "Want some?" she asked.

She skidded to a stop when she noticed the expression on Annie's face. "You're sad," she whispered, and then more loudly, "I'll get more leaves!"

Annie and Nicole both laughed.

"If only leaves could fix things." Annie sighed and closed her eyes. This day seemed as if it would never end. She was exhausted, and she wanted to go home and crawl under the scrap quilt on her bed that her *mamm* had made for her when she turned twelve.

"Does Levi know how you feel?"

"I don't even know how I feel."

"But you care for him."

Annie nodded, the misery of her situation falling on her anew.

"It'll work out."

"Don't say that."

"But it will."

"*Nein*. It won't. How can it? Levi is bound and determined to move to Texas, and more than likely he'll take you all with him."

Nicole shrugged. Earlier she had shared that they still hadn't decided whether to commit to the move. They were waiting to see what happened at Friday night's meeting.

"I can't move," Annie continued. "I won't, even if it was a possibility which it's not. After all, Levi hasn't exactly declared his love. In fact, I think he sees me as an adversary now more than ever."

"Are you?"

"Am I what?"

"His adversary."

"I don't know. I don't know what I am to him, but before the night fell apart, before Bishop Marcus came running to tell us about Old Simon... it all seemed like a dream." She rested her fingertips against her eyelids which felt swollen and warm. "I've never felt so comfortable with someone before. I've never enjoyed myself like that when I was on a date with a man—and it wasn't even a real date."

She thought of sharing the turkey leg and corn dog with Levi, and she wanted to cry all over again. If only she'd stayed home last night, maybe she wouldn't have fallen in love with him. But even as that thought entered her mind, she knew it wasn't true. Her feelings for Levi had probably begun the first day she'd seen him sitting in her parents' kitchen wearing that ridiculous Stetson.

The date the night before had simply allowed her feelings to blossom, but that would have happened regardless. It might have taken longer, but it would have happened. She didn't know when she'd become such an expert in love, but suddenly she felt as if she could write a romance story—albeit a heartbreaking one.

"Honey, listen." Micah had begun to cry, so Nicole stood, scooped him up in her arms and walked back to where Annie was sitting. "You're right. I don't know the particulars of how it can possibly work out. You and Levi always seem to be at odds with one another—your dreams for the future seem completely opposite."

"They are completely opposite."

"I think you had a dream to build a business."

"And I believe *Gotte* put that dream in my heart."

"But now I think you have a different dream—a dream of love and marriage and maybe even a family. I'm not sure that you have to give up one for the other."

"I won't do it."

"That's my point. Maybe you won't have to."

Mitchell suddenly began to cry as well. Nicole handed Micah to Annie and turned to scoop up her other son.

Annie realized in that moment just how important her niece and nephews were to her. Rachel continued to flop into the leaves—giggling, burrowing under and then popping out and shouting, "Surprise!" Micah had stopped fussing and was putting Annie's *kapp* strings in his mouth. Mitchell was sucking his thumb and snuggling close to Nicole. They were such a precious sight, so innocent and sweet and yes—beautiful—that Annie felt tears sting her eyes again.

Was this what being in love was like?

Emotions seesawing between tenderness and despair?

No wonder she'd avoided it for so long.

"I'm not saying you will or won't have to give up one dream for the other. I don't know, but I do know this. *Gotte* has a plan for you, Annie." Nicole reached over and squeezed her hand.

It wasn't lost on Annie that Levi had referred to the same verse the night before.

"And who can thwart *Gotte*'s plan? Who is big enough to do that? No one. No one can. So it will work out. Your job is to believe that, and continue to go about your day doing that day's work."

"When did you become so wise?"

"Sometime between Rachel and the twins I suppose."

Annie didn't know if she believed that things would work out. Did the Bible promise that? It seemed to her that there was a lot of heart-break and tragedy and pain in the Bible—even for *Gotte*'s people. Perhaps when they returned home, she'd spend some time reading through her favorite passages in the New Testament or the Psalms. The Psalms always calmed her heart. Maybe it was time to accept her situation and trust that *Gotte* could and would do whatever was best for her.

Chapter Eleven

For Levi, the next week was a blur of activity.

Sunday had been a visiting day, so he'd spent it at the hospital. Old Simon was improving faster than he could have imagined, and the doctors moved him into the rehab facility on Monday. Levi went about his scheduled work each day at the Kauffmanns, always arriving one to two hours early so he could tackle the day's work before the sun had even peeked over the horizon. Each day he finished by noon, and then he took the bus to Nappanee, Middlebury and Shipshewana. He met with the bishops there, shared his vision and asked them to mention the opportunity to any family who was looking to make a move. Before leaving he requested they pray for his success.

He tried to stop by the rehab facility in the late afternoon to visit Old Simon, and in the evening he would go back to Simon's house, make an egg sandwich and write letters. He wrote to anyone he had an address for. He tried to make the upcoming move sound exciting and a wonderful new opportunity and a near-certain success—and it was all those things.

But beneath all of his optimism was a kernel of doubt.

Bishop Marcus had told him to pray, and he tried. But it often felt as if his prayers stopped at the ceiling, if they even made it that far.

The bishop had also told him to look to the wisdom of family and *freinden*, but his family had already turned their backs to him. And his *freinden*? Well, that had been Annie, and he'd successfully managed to push her away.

Lastly Marcus had advised that he dedicate himself to reading scripture, and Levi tried. But each time he'd find himself staring off into space, thinking about holding Annie's hand, sharing a corn dog, hearing her laughter.

On Thursday evening, Jebediah showed up with a casserole dish that Nicole had made.

"She figured you were getting by on sandwiches."

"Pretty much."

Levi didn't bother heating the chicken casserole up. He could feel it was still lukewarm through the cloth Nicole had wrapped it in. He walked to the kitchen, fetched a fork out of the drawer, sat down at the table and dug in.

"No plate? Wow."

"You've forgotten what it's like to be a bachelor." Levi scooped up another forkful. The casserole was filled with noodles and chicken and cheese. He wasn't sure he'd ever tasted anything better in his life.

"If being a bachelor means that you eat out of the casserole dish and never clean the kitchen, I'm glad that part of my life is over." Jebediah pulled off his hat and dropped it on the table. "Nicole would be happy to get a ladies' group over here to help you clean."

"*Nein.* Old Simon won't be back for another week at the earliest. I'll have everything straightened up before then."

Jebediah clearly had his doubts. He glanced again at the sink that was overflowing with dishes, the dirty clothes that were spilling out of the mudroom and the floor that was tracked with dirt.

"Okay. If you say so."

"I do."

"You seem kind of put out. How are things going?"

"Things are going fine." Levi filled him in on all he'd done since Sunday. "I'm ready for tomorrow night's meeting. I've actually had some good results this week, better than I expected."

"So that's the reason for your good mood." Jebediah sat down across from Levi and waited.

Clearly he wasn't going to leave until he found out what was going on. Probably Nicole had sent him over to extract information, or maybe Annie had. That thought caused his mind to trip back to the night of the festival, the way her hand had felt in his, the way she'd looked at him as they'd swapped half a turkey leg for half a corndog.

Levi took a few more bites, then reached for a glass of water that had been sitting on the table and drained it. "Hopefully I'm even ready for all the negative research Annie's been doing."

"What happened to you two?"

Levi shrugged as if he had no idea what Jebediah was talking about.

"Come on. I can keep my mouth shut."

"There's nothing to tell."

"You were dating and now you're not."

"It just didn't…you know. It didn't work out."

"That's all you've got?"

"Nothing more to say." He heard the edge in his own voice and tried to lighten up a bit. "Told you I was no good with women. Maybe I'll have better luck in Texas."

"If you say so, but from my point of view you're acting like a man on a mission."

"I am."

"I didn't mean that in a *gut* way. Maybe I should have said like a crazy man on a desperate mission."

Levi looked down and realized he'd eaten half the casserole. Suddenly it felt like a brick in his stomach. He put the lid back on the dish and pushed it away.

"I'm not crazy and my mission isn't desperate."

"Have you found any ministers yet?"

"I had one call me yesterday and another send a letter. They both seem very close to committing."

"Only one to go then…"

"And three more families have signed up. If you and your *dat* would make up your minds, that would bring our total to ten."

"I'm leaning toward it, but both Nicole and I want to be very sure." He crossed his arms on the table and studied Levi. "We have *kinder*, you know."

"I'm aware."

"We can't make hasty decisions now. We need to consider a thing from all sides."

"Just come to tomorrow night's meeting. I have some *gut* news to share, and I think it might help you see things more clearly."

"Huh."

Levi stood and stretched. "I need to go muck out the barn, but thanks for bringing the food by."

"Sure." But apparently Jebediah just couldn't leave it alone. "Any message you'd like to send to Annie?"

"*Ya.* Tell her to be ready for tomorrow night, because I plan to be."

Levi was as nervous as a cat in a room full of dogs. Friday night there were even more people in attendance than at their first meeting. He kept looking out the front door, out the window, across the room. Just when he'd convinced himself that Annie wasn't going to show, she rushed through the door of Old Simon's house, breathless, clothes spattered with rain, and looking more beautiful than ever.

It took a sheer act of will to tear his eyes from her.

He needed to focus.

Tonight was important. It was crucial, and he wasn't going to let an ill-advised crush ruin his chances to finally achieve his dreams.

Annie sat in the back, between her *dat* and her *schweschder*. On the other side of Nicole was Jebediah who leaned across and said something that Annie obviously didn't like. She looked as if she was going to argue with him when Bishop Marcus stood and called the meeting to order.

"Welcome. It's *gut* to see everyone on this cold

and rainy evening. It would seem that fall has finally arrived…"

"Or winter," someone called out from the back.

"Wonder if they have this kind of weather in Texas," someone else joked.

"*Nein.* In Texas, it's always sunny." Levi couldn't resist, though the look on Annie's face made him wish he'd held his tongue.

The bishop opened the meeting with a word of prayer, asking for guidance and wisdom, and then he nodded at Levi.

"Before we begin, I'd like to update you all on Old Simon. He's been moved to the rehab center, as most of you know. Today we learned that he may be able to come home as early as the end of next week."

The news was met with nods of approval and even a few hands lifted heavenward followed by a hearty "Hallelujah."

"We would like to have a workday here on Monday," Marcus said. "We need to install some handrails and ramps. Anyone who can help, it will be much appreciated."

"What does his son Jonah say?" a man in the back asked.

"He wanted to come and see his *dat* this week, but he had to get his crop in." Levi knew that everyone in the room understood that crops couldn't wait. You helped when you could, but if at all possible crops had to come first. "He hopes to be here within the next ten days. At that point, he'll meet with Old Simon's doctors and together they will decide how best to proceed. What is certain, and I know this because I've spoken with Jonah, is that Old Simon will not be moving to Texas."

It seemed a somber note to start the meeting on, but it wasn't as if he hadn't anticipated the reaction those words would have on the group. He'd known since talking to Bishop Marcus the night in the hospital that Simon wouldn't be moving. He'd probably known it earlier when he'd spoken with the doctors, only he hadn't wanted to see it. He'd resented Marcus's brutal honesty at the time, but now he was grateful for it. The bishop had caused him to accept the way things were, deal with it and move past it.

Unfortunately, not everyone had.

Marcus was about to sit down, but he looked across the room and called on Annie. "You had a question?"

She jumped to her feet. "If we know that Old Simon can't move, and we have no other ministers who have shown an interest, what's the point in this meeting? We might as well go home."

"I was going to let Levi share this, but since you brought it up, we've actually had two ministers express a strong interest in moving to Texas."

Levi almost laughed at the look of dismay on

Annie's face. Not that he wanted her to be dismayed, but it was somewhat precious. This was turning into some sort of twisted game. She'd obviously been angry with him Saturday night, though he had no idea why. Then she had pointedly ignored him during the week, and now she seemed determined to derail his plans.

Well, he couldn't be so easily dissuaded.

He was made of tougher stuff than that.

But even as those thoughts flew through his mind, Levi met Annie's gaze and his breath caught in his chest. He saw a vulnerability in her expression that melted some of the ice around his heart. He tore his eyes away and looked down at his notes. He needed to stay focused.

"*Ya*, it's true. One minister from Shipshe and another from Ohio have expressed an interest. So we still need one more, but I feel confident we will have that commitment within a few weeks."

Annie leveled him with a pointed stare, and she only sat down when Nicole reached up and tugged on her arm.

He went on to tell the group about the letters he'd received from families who had responded to his notice in *The Budget*.

"So what you're saying is that we might have more than the dozen families?" This from Jebediah, who was holding one of the twins in his arms.

"*Ya*, if even half of the people here tonight are

serious about moving, then I'd say we have our dozen families."

Annie was on her feet again. "But what about the cost of land there? You were going to report back on that."

"Thank you, Annie, for bringing that up. I actually do have some numbers to share." The price of land was more than he had remembered, more than he had guessed, but it was still significantly less than the cost for a farm in Indiana. He spent the next ten minutes laying out the cost per acre and the amount of acreage he'd found available from a cursory search on the library's computer.

The room filled with an animated discussion of what crops would yield the most given the Texas heat.

Annie's *dat* stood and waited for everyone to quiet down. "It sounds to me that we can do this in the next few months, and though we might be late getting started on spring crops, the growing season is longer in Texas."

"It's true, but remember there is the matter of less rain so we may have to adjust our stance regarding irrigation."

"I won't abide electricity on my farm." One of the men positioned near the front of the group stood and turned to survey everyone in the room. "I personally won't have it, even if the bishop makes an allowance for such."

Levi jumped in before the discussion could be derailed with an unending wave of *what-if* scenarios. "And I respect that—however, it doesn't have to be an either/or proposition."

"What's that supposed to mean?" Annie asked.

"Simply that. There are other ways to irrigate. Advances have been made in both solar and wind energy. Water can be gathered in a cistern or from a well, and the pump can be solar or wind powered."

A discussion ensued as to the advisability of using solar power. Levi was relieved when Avery Stutzman brought up the fact that the Amish community in Colorado had allowed solar energy. He had that in his notes, but it seemed better when someone else pointed out the positive things.

He let the discussion continue for a few more minutes before he raised his hand to silence everyone.

"There is one more thing I want to bring up— something that was asked last time we met." He looked directly at Annie, who glowered back at him. Even with her eyes squinting and a frown on her lips, he thought she might be the prettiest thing he'd ever seen—prettier even than a Texas sunset.

"Actually there are two things I'd like to address. The first is whether there is a place between here and Texas where we could start a new community—a closer place. The answer to that— I realized even when Annie first asked—is of course there is. There's plenty of land between here and Texas, and no doubt some of it would be *gut* farmland. Some of it would be a fine place to build a new community. But that isn't my dream. That isn't what *Gotte* has put into my heart."

Everyone was looking at him now, but Levi didn't shy away from what he wanted to say, what he'd stayed awake the night before thinking about. "I can't say if this move is right for any of you. That's something that you have to pray about, discuss with your own families and ultimately decide for yourselves. I can only say that it is something that's been in my heart since I was a young boy."

He looked down at his notes, then folded the sheet in half. He didn't have to look at lines he'd scribbled on a sheet of paper to say what was on his mind, what filled his heart. "It could be that I made Texas into something larger than life, because I was happy there as a boy, because those years were some of the best years of my life."

The room fell silent as each person focused on Levi.

"Or it could be that it is a special place, a place where we can have room to spread out and raise our sons and daughters. So when Annie asked her second question—when she asked *why now* when it didn't work before—I had to spend a lot of time thinking about that. The only answer I've found is that now is best because it seems the time is right. To me it does, and I hope it does for you too."

He sat down then. He didn't know what else to say, how to share the feelings and thoughts and hopes and dreams that he'd carried for so long. How did a person put such things into words in a way that another person could understand? A dream shared didn't need to be explained, and a dream that wasn't shared couldn't be explained.

He couldn't look at Annie. He couldn't bear to see the disappointment in her eyes again. He understood in that moment that he had dared to hope that she would be the woman to share his dream, that she would care enough about him to come around to his point of view.

But she'd made it quite plain that such a thing wasn't going to happen.

All he had to do now was learn to live with that.

Annie's business naturally slowed down in November. Amish weddings typically took place in the spring and fall, some occurred in the summer, but very few happened between November and February. Most families began focusing on the holidays. Both Thanksgiving and Christmas were a time for family, a time to gather together, a time to pause and appreciate all that *Gotte* had done in their lives.

Also, holding an Amish wedding in the winter was complicated by the fact that it was difficult to find a place large enough to hold such a gathering once the temperatures fell to below freezing. Her business practically came to a stop when snow was on the ground. She'd never been bothered by that before. November was a good time to help her mother with canning. She also met with her business partner Priscilla once a week to go over their accounting as well as their business plans.

"I still think we should spend some of our profits on advertising," Priscilla said. "It would be nice to have more weddings scheduled, and to have families committed to using us further in advance of the actual wedding date."

"What are you going to do? Run a television ad? Amish don't watch television." Annie meant it as a joke, but her words came out with a sharp edge. They were sitting in the coffee shop in downtown Goshen, a steady rain falling outside the window. The shop was decorated with Thanksgiving decor—pumpkins and a scarecrow and even a cornucopia filled with plastic fruit. It reminded her that this was the time of year when they were supposed to be filled with gratitude.

"I was thinking more like an ad in *The Budget*, or placing flyers at local quilt shops, dry goods stores, that sort of thing."

"Uh-huh."

Priscilla tapped the table between them. "Hello! Earth to Annie."

"I'm right here." Annie turned her gaze from the harvest display to her best friend. Funny that she never would have imagined having an *Englischer* as a business partner and a friend, let alone her closest friend. *Gotte*'s ways were sometimes mysterious.

"But your mind seems to be far away. I'm going to guess your thoughts are approximately twelve hundred miles away."

Annie proceeded to crumble her scone into tiny pieces. "I'm not thinking about Levi if that's what you're saying."

"You're not?"

"Nuh-uh."

"Because I know you believe it's a sin to lie, and you wouldn't intentionally lie to me anyway since we're friends. But you might lie to yourself. That's what worries me."

Annie sank back against her chair. "They left two days ago for Texas."

"Levi and who else?"

"The minister from Shipshe…and my *bruder*."

"Ouch."

"*Ya.* My *dat* can't stop talking about it. With this rain, he has more time to read the books he continually checks out from the library, which means I'm subjected to a near-endless stream of Texas trivia. Did you know that the largest rose garden in the world is in Tyler, Texas?"

"I didn't."

"It's a big place—the Lone Star State. It holds more than seven percent of the nation's area. Hard to imagine a place that vast." She clasped her hands around her mug and finally looked up at Priscilla. "They've pretty much committed to a move in the spring."

"I'm sorry, Annie. I didn't realize things were moving so quickly."

"Indeed. Levi's a real go-getter. He could start a business moving people to Texas. Maybe the Stephenville tourism bureau would hire him."

Instead of responding to that, Priscilla sipped her coffee and allowed a moment of silence to pass between them. Annie appreciated that about her friend. Sometimes she desperately needed those moments of quiet.

They finished their drinks, bussed their table and headed outside, but they didn't immediately turn toward Priscilla's truck. Instead they stood there, pulling their coats tighter and watching the rain. Annie noticed that some of the shop windows already held Christmas displays—

snowmen, angels, Christmas trees, and brightly wrapped presents. She'd always loved Christmas, loved everything about it. She often went about humming Christmas hymns and squirreling away presents for her family.

But this year was different.

This year she wasn't feeling the joy of the season. Instead, looking at the *Englisch* displays made her heart hurt. Why did so many things cause an ache deep inside her chest?

"Have you told him how you feel?"

Annie might not have answered back in the coffee shop when she had to look Priscilla in the eye. But standing out in the rain on a cold November day, she couldn't find any good reason to avoid the subject. "I haven't. What's the point?"

"What's the point? He might feel the same, that's the point."

"If he felt the same, he wouldn't be in Texas right now, and he wouldn't be taking my family with him."

Priscilla looped her arm through Annie's and they began walking down the row of shops, under the blue canopies, toward the parking area at the end of the block. "I'm not sure that's true. It's possible to want two things at once—two things that seem completely opposed to each other."

"I guess."

"There's a reason you fell in love with him. Levi's a good person."

"I know that, and I'm not angry with him anymore."

They hurried through the rain toward the truck. Once they had fastened their seat belts and were driving through Goshen, Annie started talking, really talking, about Levi for the first time since the night they'd gone to the fall festival. She described their date, the food they'd shared, how she'd felt each time they'd held hands.

She paused to gawk at a particularly large inflatable display in an *Englisch* front yard— penguins dressed in bathing suits and holding surfboards. She wasn't sure how that related to Christmas, but it was definitely bright. Oh, and there were Christmas scarves around the penguins' necks. She pulled her attention back to Priscilla, who was still waiting for her to finish. "Did I tell you he's helping to prepare Old Simon's house for sale?"

"He is?"

"*Ya.* Old Simon had initially done well in rehab, and they thought he'd come home—even readied the house for him."

"What happened?"

"He came down with pneumonia, which he's over now, but he's weaker than before. The doctors say that he shouldn't live alone. Since Levi doesn't plan to stay here, he thought the least he could do would be to help Simon's son Jonah prepare to sell the place."

"Levi told you that?"

"*Nein*. We don't talk, not really. I heard our bishop telling my *dat*."

"What will Levi do if the farm sells before he's ready to move?"

"He says he'll move ahead of everyone else. Stay with the family who used to be their next-door neighbors, help negotiate the purchase of farms."

"The way you describe him, he sounds more like a man now, less like a boy with some crazy plan."

"*Ya*, you're right. He's changed for sure and certain."

"And you're absolutely certain that your parents are moving? They've told you that? Because sometimes your dad can be excited about a thing but not, you know, follow through."

"I haven't outright asked them."

Priscilla took her eyes off the road for a moment to give her a shocked look.

"What?" Annie shifted in her seat.

"You need to know. You need a plan."

"Uh-huh."

"Remember when you insisted we have a business plan that first year? And I just wanted to make cakes and cook and buy cool stuff."

"You had a lot of enthusiasm."

"And you had a lot of common sense. So what's happened to it?"

Instead of being offended, Annie started laughing. She could always count on Priscilla to be honest with her. "I guess I'm scared to hear what my parents will have to say. Once I know for certain, I can't un-know it."

"You also can't stick your head in the sand. Well, you can, but I don't recommend it."

They were near the farm now. When Priscilla had turned down the lane and pulled up close to the porch, she put the truck in Park and turned to study her.

"You know you could live with me, if your family moves."

"*Ya*, I know, but…"

"I'm not Amish. I'm aware." Priscilla reached over and tugged on one of her *kapp* strings. "I just want you to know you have options, until you figure out what you're going to do."

"You're a *gut* friend."

"Hey. I don't want to lose my business partner."

Annie smiled, and she actually felt a bit better for the first time in a long time. Life wasn't all gloom and doom, she realized as she dashed from the truck to her front porch. There were good people all around, and she was fortunate to have friends who cared.

Her heart might always feel bruised, but life contained other joys than romantic love. Funny thought for a wedding caterer to have, but she believed it nonetheless.

She'd nursed her hurts long enough.

As Priscilla had so aptly pointed out, it was time to take her head out of the sand. For the first time she felt like going to her bedroom and cataloging what Christmas gifts she'd purchased or made so far. They celebrated simply, swapping names among the adults and giving one gift to each grandchild, but with their growing family that still added up to quite a few gifts. She needed to make sure there was enough time left to finish up everything before the family met for the holidays. She seemed to remember a pink and purple blanket she'd started for her niece, Rachel.

Had she finished it?

Where had she put it?

Her heart still felt heavy whenever she thought of Levi, but perhaps it was time to move on. It wouldn't be a perfect Christmas, but it could still be special.

It had taken a full day's bus ride to make it from Goshen, Indiana to Stephenville, Texas. The ride was longer than it should have been because they weren't able to take a direct route. Time and again they detoured through downtown areas to drop off and pick up passengers. Still, the hours passed pleasantly enough, and Levi was able to read the book on dry-land farming in Texas that he'd borrowed from the Goshen library. They finally checked into a hotel in downtown Stephenville and slept for ten hours. The next day they spent with a Realtor, traveling from one acreage to another.

Now they were having a bite to eat at the diner attached to the hotel.

"Everything we saw today was too expensive," Adam said. He was a minister in the Shipshe district, with five young sons. He was concerned about where and how they would be able to farm, to continue their simple traditions, and he'd said more than once that he didn't want them working in the RV factory. "It's *gut* pay, but a man should be near his family, near the land, not inside a building working with machines all day."

It was a refrain that Levi had heard before, and though he had no children of his own, he understood the concern. Adam knew at least three other families who were in similar situations and had said they'd consider a move. Their numbers for the Texas settlement were growing.

"The problem is that this is horse country." Jebediah stirred a teaspoon of sugar into his coffee cup. "Instead of paying the agricultural value, owners are asking for the grazing value in an area that is apparently well-known for its horse stock."

"We wouldn't have any trouble purchasing buggy horses."

"The workhorses—now that will be a problem."

Levi heard them, but his mind was elsewhere. If he were honest with himself, which he'd been avoiding, he was thinking about Annie. Everywhere he looked there was something he wanted to show her—the quaint shops in the downtown area, the vista that stretched as far as the eye could see, the rolling hills and deep blue sky. The area was actually more picturesque than he had remembered. He had to fight the urge to call her and tell her that it was too warm to wear his jacket and that he'd seen children playing in shorts—the week before Thanksgiving.

But then maybe she would miss the snow and cold days and rain.

Why was he torturing himself this way? Annie had made it abundantly clear that she wasn't interested in moving and she wasn't interested in him.

"I need to stretch my legs," he muttered, grabbing his Stetson off the seat next to him and heading outside. He stood in the parking area for five minutes, getting his emotions under control before he turned to go back inside. As he waited for a couple in front of him to enter the café, the woman, who appeared to be in her fifties, stopped and pulled a magazine from a rack positioned outside the door. Turning to her husband, she said, "Maybe we'll find our dream place listed here."

"Anywhere you are is my dream place, darling."

Levi winced at the tender words. They would have sounded glib in any other situation, but the look on the man's face as he touched his wife's arm and held the door for her convinced Levi that the man meant every word.

Had he looked at Annie like that?

His mind flashed back to the night at the hospital, but he pushed that memory away.

Best to focus on what was possible.

He grabbed three of the magazines from the rack and carried them to the table where Jebediah and Adam were finishing up their meal.

"Have any revelations while you were out there?" Adam asked.

"Not personally, but I heard someone say they were looking for a place as they picked up these." He dropped the magazines on the table.

"Central Texas Real Estate?" Jebediah shrugged and pulled a copy closer.

Adam did the same. The conversations around

them faded into the background as they each studied the listings.

"I keep seeing listings in Hamilton, and the prices are much less expensive." Jebediah glanced up. "Any idea where that is?"

Levi turned to the map page while Adam peered over at the list that Jebediah had been studying.

"Here," Levi said. "It's less than an hour south of here."

"Do you think the Realtor will take us there?"

"It sounded like his area is primarily limited to Stephenville, and he had other appointments today." Levi waved at the waitress as she walked by with a hot pot of coffee.

"You folks need a refill?"

"*Nein*. That is, we're *gut* as far as coffee. I was wondering if you could tell us how to get to Hamilton."

"Oh, that's easy. You get on Highway 281, which veers right when you reach Hico. Keep heading south and you'll be there in no time."

"We're visiting from out of town. We don't have a vehicle…"

Jebediah laughed at that. "And we're Amish, so we wouldn't own one even if we lived here."

"I thought you might be," she said with a smile.

"The suspenders and beards must have been a dead giveaway," Jebediah joked.

"Pretty much. My aunt lives in Pennsylvania, and I stayed with her a few summers." She pulled a cell phone out of her apron pocket. "I know you don't own phones, so you can use mine if you want."

"And call whom?"

"Uber, of course."

Fifteen minutes later, they were headed south.

Chapter Twelve

Annie planned all afternoon what she wanted to say to her parents, but she waited until they'd all sat down for supper. Her *dat* looked tired from his long day working in the barn, and her *mamm* had spent the afternoon helping a neighbor who had fallen and broken her leg. She let them talk about their day, remembered to ask the occasional question and tried to actually eat the ham, potatoes, corn and fresh bread on her plate.

She succeeded marginally.

If they noticed, no one said anything.

Finally, her *dat* pushed his plate away and reached for his coffee cup.

"Let me refill that." Annie jumped up and filled both his cup and her *mamm*'s.

They shared a look which said they knew something was up, but waited for her to take her seat again and clasp her hands in front of her.

When she couldn't seem to find the words to start, her *mamm* reached toward her and brushed her *kapp* string back, as she'd done when Annie was a small child, as she'd done a million times. "Did you want to talk to us about something, dear?"

"*Ya.* Actually, I did. I wanted to ask, that is, I'd like to know your intentions regarding moving."

Her *mamm* looked to her *dat* as if she were passing the ball to him. That was when Annie knew her fate was sealed. They'd already decided. They'd spoken about it, perhaps when she was sitting in this very room but too absorbed by her own problems to pay any attention to them.

Her *dat* sipped his coffee, took his time framing his answer. "Your *schweschder...*"

"Nicole?"

"*Ya.* Both she and Jebediah are worried about the cost of land here—he's worried his boys won't be able to afford it and that his girls will have to move away in order to marry and start a family."

"Plenty of young people marry and stay in the area."

"True, but how many of those couples are living on their parents' land? Not that Jebediah would mind that, and he certainly has many years before the boys are ready to marry..."

"The twins haven't turned one yet," she whispered.

"Next month," her *mamm* said. "I understand

his concerns must seem premature to you, but trust me, the years will fly by. Plus, a move will be easier while the children are young."

"It doesn't mean *you* have to go."

"*Nein.* We don't have to, but we feel the Lord calling us to do so." Her *mamm*'s voice was gentle but firm.

"So it's decided? You are going?"

Her *dat* nodded and though he was probably trying to contain his enthusiasm for her sake, he didn't quite succeed. A smile spread across his face, and he began drumming his fingertips against the tabletop. "We'll wait and hear the report, but if there's affordable land to purchase, then *ya*. We will be moving when your *schweschder* does."

The words sliced through her heart, but she had a moment of clarity at the same time. She could fight this and be miserable for the time they had left or she could accept the situation for what it was. In some strange way she also felt lighter from hearing their plans. The worst had come about. She could stop worrying and start dealing with it.

"I plan to stay."

Her *mamm* reached for her hand and covered it with her own. "Your older *bruders* and *schweschder* will still be in the area, for now, and they've all said they'd be happy to have you live with them."

It had gone that far?

They'd decided where she was going to live?

Annie felt her old stubbornness rise, and it was like a coat that she'd pushed to the back of the closet and just recently rediscovered. She was tired of crying, tired of worrying, and suddenly she knew that she would find a way to deal with this and she'd do so on her own terms.

"Priscilla said that I could live with her."

Her *dat* stared into his coffee cup. When he glanced up, she saw nothing but concern in his eyes, and she felt bad for causing them so much worry.

"She's a *gut* person. You both know that. You both like her."

"You're not thinking of leaving the faith, are you?" Her mother watched her carefully.

"*Nein*. I like being Amish. I am Amish, but I need somewhere to live, and our catering business is really taking off. I don't want to move to Shipshe or Middlebury. I like it here." She realized the absurdity of that. Her parents were going to move twelve hundred miles away, and she was insisting that a ten-mile change would be too much. "I know I don't need your permission, but I'd like your blessing."

"That you will always have, Anna Marie." Her

dat so rarely used her full name that it always brought a lump to her throat. The words were like a caress and a blessing all in one.

Her *mamm* stood, began picking up dishes and then paused to kiss Annie on the top of the head. "You must promise to come and visit us—at least twice a year."

"*Ya*, of course."

"And who knows, maybe when you do, you'll like it enough to stay."

Annie didn't think that was likely.

She could only imagine how terrible it would be to visit her family in their new home, meet neighbors that she didn't know and hadn't grown up with, continue to see Levi after he settled down and married. *Nein*, she did not picture herself visiting Texas twice a year. But she didn't voice her concerns. Now wasn't the time. She had moved from grieving into planning in the space of a heartbeat.

"Have you talked about a date...for the move?"

She hadn't attended the last two meetings regarding the Texas settlement, and she'd avoided being alone with Nicole. She hadn't been able to bear her *schweschder*'s talk of a new life. Now she regretted the distance she'd put between them, and she vowed to spend as much time as possible with her niece and nephews in the next few months.

"We'll go in the spring, if Levi and Jebediah have been able to locate farms we can afford to purchase. It could be as late as summer if it takes a long time to sell this place."

They all knew that wasn't likely.

The reason they were moving was because there were more people who wanted to buy land in the area than there was land for sale. The farm was tidy and profitable. It would probably sell as soon as they stuck a sign in the ground. This time next year her family would be celebrating Christmas in Texas, and she would be here.

Alone.

Levi, Jebediah and Adam stood at the crest of a hill, an elderly *Englisch* farmer at their side. Buddy Johnston had just celebrated his eighty-eighth birthday. He was nearly as round as he was tall, but he had the hands and the bearing of a farmer.

"It's *gut* land," Jebediah said.

"Yes, it is, and it pains me to sell it." Buddy hooked his thumbs under his belt and shrugged. "My boys, they all work in the city now. They're not farmers, and neither of them has any use for this place. Also they could use the money from the sale—though they're in no hurry for it. Still, when me and Betty pass on, the money will be a nice amount to give to them."

"Hopefully that won't be anytime soon," Levi said.

"Eh. It's in the Lord's hands, and I'm good with that."

Which seemed to confirm that this was a place they were meant to be, on land that had been farmed by a God-fearing man, passed on to God-fearing men. It didn't always happen that way, but when it did Levi sensed a special blessing.

"Would you mind if we took a moment to speak among ourselves?" Adam asked.

"Take your time, and join me for some of Betty's coffee and pecan pie when you're done. Trust me. Betty's pie is not something you want to miss."

They watched him toddle down the lane which led to the house. An old hound dog had been lying in the sun, but it jumped up and trotted over to walk beside him, something they'd probably done together a thousand times.

"Should one of us go with him, make sure he doesn't fall?" Jebediah was like that—a caretaker in more ways than one.

"He's been walking this farm longer than the three of us have been alive," Adam said. "I think he'll be fine."

They turned and stared out at the land, which

stretched to the horizon. There was a high plateau to the east. They could just make out a cut between the hills, which was the road they'd travelled on from Stephenville. What might have been the remnant of an ancient volcano shimmered to the south, and farmland as far as you could see spread to the west.

"This is a big place." Adam turned in a circle, trying to take it all in.

"A thousand acres—" Levi pulled off his hat and held it in both hands. "It could be divided into ten, maybe eleven farms."

"We have fourteen families," Jebediah pointed out.

"And we passed three other farms for sale on our way here."

"Speaking of which…" Adam glanced back toward the farmhouse. "How are we going to get the Uber driver back?"

"I paid him twenty dollars to go to town and get dinner. He had a few errands to run and said he'd be back here by dark."

The three fell silent, each contemplating the enormity of the decision they were about to make.

"We've been given the duty of finding land for our community. It's a solemn and weighty thing to make such a decision, and it's important that we be in complete agreement." Adam fell into the role of leader easily.

Levi thought he'd make a good bishop, a fair one who would make the physical and spiritual health of their community his priority.

"Any hesitation, any doubt at all—now is the time to voice it."

"I can't think of any reason not to make this deal." Jebediah pulled his gaze from the horizon and nodded at Levi. "Can you?"

"*Nein*. It's all I've dreamt of, all I've hoped and prayed for."

"Then we're in agreement," Adam said.

"*Ya*, I'm in agreement." Jebediah shoved his hands into his pockets, a smile spreading across his face. "I can see my boys growing up here. The land is less expensive than Stephenville, the barns not as well cared for, but we can easily rebuild a barn."

Levi had waited for this moment for so long that he felt a lump rise in his throat. "*Ya*, I agree," he said, which seemed to be all there was to say. He was aware that with those words, he not only changed the direction of his own life, but he also was changing the lives of all of the families who would be moving. And of course it would affect one pretty young lady who would not be coming to Texas.

Why was life so full of difficult decisions?

Why were his feelings for Annie so strong at a

time when he should be focused on this land and the families he had committed to bringing here?

He knew in his heart that this move was good and right and something they should do. For Levi, it was like coming home again, the fulfillment of years' worth of planning and working.

So why, when they turned toward the house, to tell Buddy Johnston and his wife that they'd gladly purchase their land at the suggested price, did his heart ache with another dream that died even as this one was born?

Thirty minutes later, Buddy's neighbor had arrived. The man also happened to be his lawyer.

"We called him while you were surveying the place," Buddy explained. "Seemed to me that you liked it."

"This is a preliminary notice of intention to purchase that I downloaded from the internet." Raymond Cole was probably in his fifties, had the soft, cultured voice of a man with an advanced education and the calluses of a farmer. His skin was ebony black, his hair graying at the temples, and his manner serious.

"We would have been happy with a handwritten receipt and a handshake," Adam said.

"And it says something about you folks that you would have been." Raymond accepted the three copies that they all had signed and added his own signature under the word *Witness*. "I'm not sure I'd recommend carrying twenty thousand dollars in earnest money around in your pocket, but it certainly speeds things up that we don't have to wait three days for a transfer of funds."

"We wanted to be able to show that we were serious about our ability to purchase such a large parcel."

"I say it's time to celebrate." Betty set the pecan pie in the middle of the table. Like Buddy, she was in her eighties. Her hair was whiter than the cotton they'd seen in the fields on the drive down, and her skin thin as parchment. Whereas Buddy was short and round, Betty's build was slight and her posture ramrod straight. They both seemed at peace with the decision to move off the farm.

Levi glanced around the kitchen, saw a rocking chair in the corner and beside it a small table with an open Bible resting on it. So they were truly people of faith. That might explain their calm and confident nature. He remembered Buddy's comment, *It's in the Lord's hands, and I'm good with that*. What more could a person ask for than to be at peace with the Lord's guidance in their life?

The pie had already been sliced into pieces. Betty placed a tray with six mugs, sugar, cream and a pot of coffee in the middle. "You folks help yourself."

"Where will you go?" Levi asked.

"Our sons have already picked out a place in

Sun City—it's a development for old folks, but they have a fine golf course there."

"And is it closer to your sons?" Jebediah asked.

"Yes, it is. Our oldest has three pretty grand-babies, and they live in Georgetown. We'll be able to see them as often as we want. At our age, that's more important than having a field to plant winter oats in."

Levi had enjoyed Mrs. Calloway's pecan pie growing up, and Betty's was every bit as good as hers. He couldn't help laughing when Jebediah took his first bite.

"Your eyes nearly rolled up in your head."

"This is as good as shoofly pie. I didn't think anything was as good as that."

"Your wife and I will have to swap recipes, in that case. Buddy's never had shoofly pie."

"Doctor says I'm supposed to cut back, but then he's never tried Betty's cooking or he wouldn't ask me to do such a thing."

There was talk of farming and families and the upcoming Thanksgiving holiday. When they'd all finished their pie, Raymond sat forward, cross-ing his arms on the table and looking at each of them in turn. Levi had the sense that this was the real test—not how much money they had or their knowledge of farming.

Raymond was assessing them.

If they were found wanting, in his estimation,

then their time in Texas would be difficult because word would spread. Call it gossip or call it being neighborly, one man talks to another who then talks to another. It was the way of things, and Levi didn't hold it against the man, though he did hope that they'd pass with flying colors.

"I've read a little about you people."

"Have you now?" Adam nodded as if it had been wise for Raymond to check them out before accepting their money. "And do you have any questions?"

"I do."

"Fire away."

"Is it true that you have extremely large families?"

"It is."

"Eight to ten children?"

"Not unusual."

Levi nodded, but it was Jebediah who jumped into the conversation.

"My wife and I have a three-year-old girl and twin boys who will turn one next month…"

Raymond let out a long whistle.

"And they're expecting another," Levi added.

Raymond's eyebrows shot up. "Four children under four? Is that normal?"

"It's not unusual."

Adam nodded toward the Bible that sat near the rocker. Levi wondered if Betty had been doing some reading before they all traipsed in. He marveled again that they would be buying the land from fellow believers of God's word. "Our understanding of the Scripture teaches us that the Lord grows each household as He sees fit."

"I was one of ten," Buddy commented.

Betty added, "It was normal in our generation, but our children all think that two or three are a handful, and perhaps in this day and age, in our modernized way of life, perhaps they're right."

Raymond nodded as if that all made sense and moved on to his next question. "You're not allowed to use technology—cars or electricity or computers?"

"It's true that we prefer the old ways," Adam said. "Though it's not a matter of being allowed so much as it is that we prefer to not have the distractions of a television set or the expense of an automobile. Each community has its own guidelines. For instance, we may decide that solar energy would be beneficial, even necessary, in order to irrigate our crops."

It seemed to be a good enough answer for Raymond who nodded and then distributed the copies of the papers they'd signed and slipped his into a battered old leather bag.

Levi wasn't sure if they'd passed the test until they were all walking out to the front porch and

Raymond said, "How much more land do you think you'll need?"

"At this point—two or three hundred additional acres."

"I think I know two other families who would be interested in selling. Their land is close to here. One is a hundred and twenty acres. The other is a hundred and thirty. If you'd like, I could contact them."

"*Ya*, we'd like that," Adam said.

Levi released a breath he didn't realize he'd been holding. Finally he dared to believe it was actually going to happen—after twelve long years he was moving back to Texas.

Annie was sitting at the kitchen table planning their Thanksgiving dinner when Nicole arrived with the news. Jebediah had left a message at the phone shack. They'd found land. Soon Annie's *dat* and *mamm* were gathered around the table, and they were all studying a map of Texas. They wouldn't be living in Levi's beloved Stephenville, but they'd be close. She could only imagine how happy he was.

The next week both farms went up for sale, and Annie helped her sister make lists of what she needed to pack in what order, what could be sold and what would need to be purchased in Texas versus what should be moved. The horses would stay. There simply wasn't an economical way to move them, but they'd have good homes. That was one thing for certain—as long as there was an Amish community nearby, any horse would have a home.

Annie wondered if they would move before Nicole gave birth. She'd been present when Rachel, Micah and Mitchell were born. She'd presumed she would be there for all of her *schweschder*'s births, but in the future she would have to be satisfied with reading about them in letters and the occasional visit.

Her *dat* was over the moon with enthusiasm. She'd never seen him so focused. Her *mamm* had been right, and even Annie could see it. The move was going to be good for him. Sometimes change was exactly what the doctor ordered. Sometimes change was what you needed when you didn't even realize you needed anything.

Moving plans halted long enough for them to prepare for Thanksgiving. All of her siblings and their families would be coming as well as Levi. Annie had done her best to avoid him, and she hoped the size of the crowd at her house would negate any awkward feelings.

But as soon as he walked inside, sporting his Stetson and those old cowboy boots which she noticed he had at least bothered to shine, she walked straight up to him. What was the point in remaining angry? Soon he'd be gone, and she would wish that she had settled things between them.

"Congratulations. You're going home to Texas."

The room was crowded with family, children running in circles and a large number of coats and scarves and gloves and mittens piled on the pegs near the front door. He pulled her out onto the porch. A light snow was falling, and she realized with a start that Christmas was just around the corner. It made her feel both amused and sad that she'd thought she could be a matchmaker for Levi. She'd thought she could have him promised off to another woman by Christmas.

"Are you sure you won't go with us?" Levi asked, staring at her, watching for any sign of hesitation.

"*Nein*, but I'm happy for you."

He didn't smile, didn't respond to that remark at all. Instead he turned and placed his hands on the porch railing and stared out at the fields that were slowly turning white.

"What's wrong?"

He shook his head, reminding her of their workhorse Pretty Boy, tossing his mane as he headed across the field.

"Isn't this what you wanted?"

"Yes and no."

"I don't understand."

"Neither do I."

And then he turned to look at her, his eyes searching her face as he stepped closer.

She stepped back. Heat crept up her neck. She wiped her sweating palms on her apron, and wondered if she might be coming down with something.

And why was Levi watching her so intently?

What was he trying so hard not to say?

Levi cleared his throat. "I guess I didn't account for all that would happen to me when I moved here to Goshen."

"Is that so?"

"It is."

"I hope they were *gut* things."

"The verdict's still out."

"Anything I can help you with?"

Her heart had started thumping like the drummers in the Goshen High School band in the Christmas parade. She clutched her hands in front of her, not because she was afraid but because she had the sudden urge to reach out and touch him before he disappeared like a mirage that she couldn't prove had ever been there.

Levi stepped closer, ducked his head, and she had the startling realization that he was going to kiss her when the front door burst open and three of her nephews tumbled out—laughing and running and determined to make snowballs out of the slight amounts of snow.

"I better go and help Mamm," she murmured, her cheeks burning and her voice sounding like someone else completely.

He stepped back, smirked, and tipped his hat.

That hat!

It brought her to her senses faster than anything else could have.

Levi Lapp was determined to be a cowboy, and to think that he had any other plans at all—that was the way of folly.

Dinner was a boisterous affair that they held in the barn on tables made from sawhorses.

It had been this way for years—as their family had grown, as the children had multiplied until it seemed they could fill a one-room schoolhouse with the Kauffmann family alone.

She'd hoped they could enjoy the food with no mention of the move, but it was on everyone's mind, and her *dat* addressed it before the first bite was taken.

After their silent prayer, he stood, his head still bowed, and she realized how much she loved this man who had raised her, how much she respected him and how much she would miss him.

"*Gotte*, we thank You for all the *gut* things You have provided us—for the food on this table, for the daughters and sons, grandchildren and *freinden* around it. We thank You for the ultimate gift of our Lord and Savior Jesus Christ, and Father we thank You for the dreams You have put in our hearts. We ask that as we begin to make our way on this grand adventure, that You will guide our every step, that You will provide our safety and that You will hold our hearts together as one."

Amens rippled around the table, but Annie had to stare at her lap, tears pricking her eyes, and her *dat*'s words, *hold our hearts together as one*, echoing through her heart.

The rest of the meal passed in a flurry of laughter and good-natured teasing. The adults spoke of the move. The children talked of Christmas and the upcoming holiday from school. If she closed her eyes, Annie could almost pretend it was a normal Thanksgiving meal. It was followed by dessert and games and more food to set out for dinner.

If she'd thought that she had successfully managed to avoid Levi Lapp, she was sorely mistaken. It was nearly evening when she stepped out the back door to look up at the stars. The snow had stopped. The clouds had moved off to the east and left behind a scene that looked like something from a child's storybook.

"Beautiful, isn't it?"

Annie jumped, a squeal escaping her lips.

"Didn't mean to scare you."

"I thought I was alone." She raised her chin, feeling ridiculous but needing to at least appear to have control of her emotions. Pulling her coat more tightly about her, she marched out to the swing, hoping Levi would take the hint and allow her some time alone.

He didn't.

Instead he sat next to her and set the swing in motion.

"Do you need a little time alone?"

"It was a goal."

"You have a lot of nephews and nieces."

"And I love every one of them."

"But…"

She couldn't help laughing. "They're a rowdy bunch. I'm not quite used to that much motion and commotion."

"Timothy put a snowball down the back of my shirt."

"Did he now?" She'd have to be sure and give Timothy an extra cinnamon roll in the morning.

"Deborah insisted I sit in a barn stall and hold the newborn kittens."

"She's a precious one."

"Did you know she's named all nine of them?"

"I'm not surprised."

"I like your family, Annie."

Well, you can't have them.

The thought popped into her mind, and she

instantly regretted it. Levi cared for her family, and they cared for him. Her father had accepted him as a son; that much was obvious.

"Do you miss your family?" she asked.

"I suppose, but being here…it helps me to realize how unhealthy, how unnatural that situation has been and continues to be. I can only hope and pray that they find a way to love one another, a way to forget the hurts of the past."

"You could pray for them."

"I do, and I write to them. Not enough, but I plan to do better."

They sat in silence for a while, and Annie felt the tension inside of her unwind like a child's rope swing. The night was cold but not bitterly so. The stars sparkled as if the light winter storm had brushed the dust away and left them with freshly cleaned constellations. A slight moon shone across the snow-covered fields. She could just make out tracks leading from the back door to the barn, no doubt momma cat in search of her evening meal.

She sighed, her heart both happy and hurting at the same time.

"I'm going to miss it here when I move to town."

"I know you will—and I'm sorry, I really am—for any grief that my actions, my dreams have brought to your life."

When he placed his hand over hers, she nearly catapulted off the swing. But his apology seemed sincere.

"Danki," she whispered.

"You won't consider going with us?"

"Nein. I need to be here."

"What if…what if you met someone, fell in *lieb…"*

"If I did…" She looked at him then, thinking that she'd never seen eyes so kind and so troubled at the same time. "If I did, he would understand."

"Understand what?"

"That I need to be here, at least for now."

The last wedding of the year was the second weekend in December. Widow Schwartz was marrying Clyde Gold. Annie kept referring to her as Widow Gold, which made Levi laugh every time.

"Neither has exactly stored up a pile of money," he'd explained when Annie had finally asked him why he was laughing. "I just find the name Gold funny and a little ironic for Amish folk."

Annie shook her head. "Keep acting silly and you won't receive a single Christmas present."

"Does that mean I *am* receiving a present?"

Instead of answering, she'd given him a pointed look and sauntered off. He thought of the snow globe he'd purchased for her in Texas. Inside the globe was a field of Texas bluebonnets, and when you shook it, they became covered with snow.

Since that night on the swing, there had been a change in Annie's attitude. She'd settled somewhere between the sweet girl he'd taken to the fall festival and the frightened woman who had tried to stop the move. He spent every free moment he could find around her, trying to soak in her Annie-ness. Trying to store up enough memories to get him through the year ahead until she came to visit her parents.

Things were changing quickly in their community.

Old Simon's place had sold, and Levi was now living with Bishop Marcus.

He'd rather have stayed with Annie's family.

He wanted time to be with her, to persuade her that they could have a future together.

She'd seemed to at least consider the idea on Thanksgiving night as they'd sat on the swing. Each evening as he went to sleep, that was the thing he thought of—not Texas, which had once been so important to him, and it still was. It was hard to admit that the idea of moving didn't bring the excitement and joy it once had.

Was that how life was?

You worked for and sought after a thing and then when you achieved it, the thing didn't matter as much?

Or was something else happening here?

Had he fallen in love with Annie Kauffmann?

And if he had, what was he going to do about it?

He realized with a start that she was talking about the upcoming wedding and he hadn't heard a word.

"I'm surprised they're even having a wedding celebration," he blurted out.

Annie was helping him brush down the horses. She'd taken to doing it every evening since the Thanksgiving dinner, and it certainly wasn't necessary. He'd told her so every night that he worked at their farm, and every night she'd insisted that she needed time out of the house. All day he looked forward to these moments they shared together, even if there was a nine-hundred-pound horse between them.

"Why would you be surprised?"

"They're so old."

"Younger than my parents."

"Still."

"What would you have them do? Amish don't elope."

He rubbed his jawline as if he needed to seriously consider the idea. "They could. They could ask the bishop to say a few words of blessing, then slip off to Niagara Falls for a little vacation. No need for all the fuss and planning."

"Hey. That's my job you're doing away with."

She smiled at him, and Levi lost another piece of his heart.

He'd thought of skipping the wedding. There was still much to do to get ready for the move. At the moment, he was trying to negotiate the shipment of a dozen buggies, which was difficult enough. Explaining that they needed to be left at Buddy and Betty's farm, where no one was currently living, was even harder.

But a clock had begun to tick in his mind, a countdown clock of how many days he had left with Annie.

For sure and certain he would go to the wedding.

Chapter Thirteen

It was a cold, blustery day so the festivities were held in the barn on the Saturday before Christmas. It was Annie's last wedding until March. She'd told Levi that she would focus on helping her *mamm* to pack and moving her own things to town.

The weather certainly wasn't unusual for December in Indiana, but the wedding venue? He'd never seen anything like it. He'd come to accept that Annie rarely did things in a usual way—the rustic setting hadn't stopped her from decorating as if they were spread across a majestic lawn. There was more greenery inside the barn than out, plus the addition of pinecones filled the air with a nice woodsy scent. Add to that miles and miles of some kind of sheer fluffy white fabric wrapped around anything that wasn't moving and you had a pretty swanky setting.

The ceremony was simple with only a few songs and a short sermon by Bishop Marcus. Levi had mocked the thought of the older couple having a wedding, but seeing them stand at the front of the crowd tugged at his heart and twisted something in his gut. The way they looked at each other, the years fell away and they were simply a man and a woman in love.

They were pronounced husband and wife to much cheering and clapping, and then everyone began moving the benches to where tables had been made out of planks and sawhorses. They were adorned with white tablecloths and small jars of fragrant cedar mixed with white carnations. Fragrant holly berries had been woven like a ribbon along the length of the tables. It reminded him of Christmas, the last holiday he would spend in Goshen. He was moving to Texas after the first of the year.

Tiny lights sparkled along the rafters of the barn.

"How'd she do that?" he asked Nicole.

"The lights? Annie purchased a generator that they carry in the back of the wedding trailer."

The wedding trailer—something he'd laughed at the first day he'd arrived at her parents' farm. Now it was pulled up next to Clyde Gold's barn. When Levi went outside and looked, an extension cord ran from the trailer toward the barn.

"Next thing we know you're going to hire a string quartet," he teased as Annie popped out of the trailer juggling two trays of food. "Let me take those."

He spent the next half hour helping to carry food into the barn.

"We might need to hire him," Priscilla quipped.

But it wasn't until the meal was over and the happy couple was preparing to leave on their short honeymoon—to Sarasota, Florida, not Niagara Falls—that Levi managed to catch a few minutes alone with Annie.

She was standing at the far end of the barn, arms crossed, surveying the crowd.

"*Gut* wedding."

"*Ya.*" She continued watching the group, but finally she sighed and turned toward him. "It's been a *gut* year. Lots of happy couples now sharing cozy little homes, starting new lives together, and some of them are already having babies."

"We could do that."

For a moment he feared that she would laugh at him, but then her expression turned tender and she reached out and tapped the top of his Stetson.

"Long-distance romances rarely work. Long-distance marriages surely wouldn't."

"Come to Texas with me."

"I can't, Levi. I can't do that."

He'd expected that answer, but he'd also feared

she would deny having any feelings whatsoever for him.

So instead of focusing on the negative, he stepped closer, waited for her to look up at him, and then he did what he'd wanted to do since that first night when he'd sat on the steps of her trailer. He kissed her, and she tasted like summertime and lemonade and pecan pie.

She didn't move away, so he touched her face with his fingertips and kissed her again.

Finally she began to laugh, and stepped away.

"You are one bold cowboy."

"Or a desperate one."

"I have to go. Night falls early, and Priscilla and I still have to pack up everything."

"I'll help."

But for a moment they simply stood there, as he drank in the sight of her, fearing she might disappear if he dared to look away. He was a man dying of thirst, and the only things that could slack it, the only things that could ease the ache in his throat, were Annie's smile, Annie's touch, Annie standing next to him. She caught him staring, and he held out his hand, held it out between them, palm up.

She placed her hand in his, and they turned and walked back toward the group. Levi had the strangest sensation that she'd done so much more than put her hand in his, that she'd finally put her trust in him. Her words had said one thing but her actions and her expression—well they had said something completely different.

As clearly as if she'd spoken the words, he heard, *Levi, I trust you to find a way to make this work.*

And the fear and the loss and the ache that he'd been dealing with since that night in October when he'd sat in the hospital not knowing Old Simon's condition, those things melted away as if they'd never existed.

Once they'd packed everything up, Levi followed behind Annie's wedding trailer. He was driving Old Simon's buggy again, because it still didn't make sense to purchase his own, especially given the impending move. There were days though, when he was tempted. Old Petunia wasn't exactly spry. Sometimes he feared the mare would fall asleep in the middle of the road. So it was that he was lagging a bit behind.

He caught the light that Priscilla sailed through and more cars turning from the cross street filled the space between them.

It wasn't like he didn't know where they were going—Priscilla was driving the trailer back to Annie's farm. They would store it there until spring when they would move it to a storage facility they'd checked into renting. They definitely couldn't park it at the duplex where Priscilla lived—where Annie planned to live.

Levi had offered to follow them because he wanted more time with Annie. He wanted to explain what he'd meant when he'd said he was desperate.

He hadn't planned on saying that. The words had slipped out of his mouth before he'd considered how they'd affect her. Or maybe he hadn't thought they would.

Did she care about him?

Did she want him to stay?

Did she expect him to give up his dream of Texas?

And beneath those questions, a more important one…would she ever consider moving with him?

He pulled in a deep breath, certain he was building castles in the sand. There was no way that Annie Kauffmann was falling for him. He'd be better off forgetting the kiss they'd shared, the way she'd looked up at him in the moonlight, the ache in his chest when he thought about leaving.

He'd be better off sticking to his original plan.

Or would he?

Glancing out the buggy's window, he saw a man dressed in a Santa Claus costume walking into a bookstore where a group of children were waiting.

Children's wishes were so simple—a new doll, a baseball bat, maybe a set of clothing.

What Levi wished for, what he desperately wanted for Christmas, was Annie by his side for the rest of his life. But how could he ask her that? How could he ask her to give up everything she'd worked so hard to build?

The traffic had begun to move, and Levi was thinking about all of the questions circling his brain and the confusing turns his life seemed to take, when he heard a thunderous crash. He glanced around, uncertain what had happened. Then the car in front of him slammed on its brakes. Levi jerked hard on Petunia's reins, and she stopped so abruptly that he was thrown forward in the seat.

"Whoa. Easy, girl. It's all right."

But it wasn't all right. He realized that several people were screaming, and they were all running forward, running toward the intersection that was up ahead. Some people slammed their car doors shut, while others simply abandoned their vehicles. Everyone was streaming forward in the direction of the next block.

He attempted to guide Petunia forward, but the traffic was at a halt. He jumped out of the buggy and climbed up on the hitch, attempting to see.

"What is it?" he asked an *Englischer* who was hurrying back in his direction.

"Eighteen wheeler sideswiped another vehicle. Ambulance and fire truck are on the way."

"Vehicle…what type of vehicle?"

"Some kind of truck," the man said. "White, I think. It was pulling a large trailer. There's debris all over the intersection. A doctor who saw it happen is working on the woman…"

Levi didn't stay to hear another word.

He scrambled up into the buggy, threw on the brake, called out to the mare and vaulted out of the buggy, leaving the door wide open.

An accident.

White truck and trailer.

Debris everywhere.

And a doctor working on a woman.

"Please, *Gotte*, please…" The cry of his heart rose up into his throat. As he pushed his way through the bystanders, he heard someone say, "I need you people to step back and give the doctor some room."

He saw the words *Plain & Simple Weddings* on the side of the trailer.

His hands began to shake and a buzzing noise filled his head.

The trailer—Annie's trailer—was barely distinguishable as such. The impact of the semi into the truck had caused the trailer to jackknife. It lay on its left side, the doors thrown open, the sidewall crushed. Plates and dishes and food littered the road as if someone had tossed everything out of the trailer.

But he didn't care about any of that.

Legs trembling, he pushed forward.

Now he could see what had happened. Priscilla had pulled into the intersection and her truck had been hit by the eighteen wheeler. The truck had broken away from the trailer, spun around and was now facing back toward the way it had come. He could see the shattered windshield. Someone was helping Priscilla out of the driver's seat. She was in obvious pain, holding her arm at an awkward angle, but she was able to walk with assistance.

Levi pushed through the crowd to the other side of the truck—the side that had taken the brunt of the collision.

Annie had been pulled from the wreckage and laid out on the street. A man knelt beside her, one hand on her wrist.

"Has anyone called 911?" The doctor's voice was calm, but the expression on his face said everything—lines drawn between his eyes, attention focused on Annie.

"They're two minutes away," someone said.

"I saw it happen. The semi sailed through the red light, didn't even slow down."

"It's a miracle she's alive."

Levi heard all of these things, but his mind

couldn't grasp and hold on to them. He only knew that it was Annie who was in danger. It was Annie that he had to get to.

Forcing his way through the crowd, he crouched next to the doctor.

"Annie. Annie, can you hear me?" He reached out, touched her hair where the *kapp* had slipped away, prayed that she would open her eyes.

"Do you know her?"

"*Ya*. Her name's Annie, Annie Kauffmann. Is she…"

He couldn't say the word, could barely see through the tears that he swiped away.

"Look at me. Sir, look at me." The doctor's eyes were compassionate, understanding. "She's hurt, but help is on the way. She's unconscious at the moment. Do you know if she has any underlying health conditions?"

"Underlying?"

"Epilepsy, heart condition, pregnancy…anything the paramedics should know about."

"*Nein*. Nothing like that."

Annie's eyes remained closed. She almost looked as if she was sleeping, except for the cut on her forehead, the blood trickling down her face and the way her legs were splayed at an unnatural angle. He glanced over at Priscilla's truck, trying to comprehend that she'd been sitting beneath what was now wreckage.

How had she survived?

Sirens split the afternoon, and then they were surrounded by paramedics insisting that he step back. A fire truck arrived. Before he could comprehend what had happened, they'd placed her on a gurney, covered her with a blanket and the ambulance had sped away.

He reached out for the arm of the man who had been checking her vitals. "Where will they take her?"

"To the hospital here in Goshen. Do you need a ride?"

"Nein. I have a buggy." Which was when he realized he'd left Petunia in the middle of the road. He jogged back toward the buggy to find that it was gone. An Amish woman—he couldn't remember if he had met her before or if she was even a member of their congregation—waved at him.

"My husband saw what happened. He moved your buggy around the corner. That way."

"Danki." He took off at a jog and had no problem spotting the rig a block down the road and on the right.

"We saw the accident," the man said as he approached. "Annie was in the truck?"

So they were a part of their congregation, or maybe they knew her from a wedding they'd attended.

"Ya, she's hurt and so was the driver, Priscilla.

Annie was unconscious. They're taking her to the hospital. I'm going to follow."

"We'll call the bishop and her parents."

"Danki." The words were perfunctory, but he realized he meant them. He was grateful that he didn't have to stop to make a call, didn't have to slow down for even that important errand, because the only thing that mattered was getting to the hospital. The only thing he cared about was Annie and being with her.

Annie woke to the noise of machinery she couldn't identify. There was a swoosh-swoosh sound and a feeling that someone was gripping her arm. She wanted to ask if Levi was there, but she couldn't form the words to do so. Another machine beeped. Soft footsteps echoed close by. She tried to open her eyes, but her eyelids were so incredibly heavy.

Perhaps if she slept a little longer...

Annie stared at a yard full of wedding decorations—the tables covered with cloth and sporting spring flowers and cats. There seemed to be cats everywhere. They wound their way down the tables, stopped to sniff at the celery in the mason jars, batted at the flowers. One large tabby collapsed on the bride's table as if the place had been decorated particularly for his benefit.

Levi laughed and said, "We grow them bigger

in Texas. Most cats there are the size of mountain lions."

Were there mountain lions in Texas?

Were there mountain lions at this wedding?

She couldn't think about that. She needed to get rid of the cats. She'd shoo away one, and it would be replaced by three more. Where had they all come from? And why couldn't she reach out and pick one up? Then the rain started, and the cats began to meow and brush up against her legs. Finally they settled, a nice warm pressure, comforting in a purring kind of way.

She knew that she needed to get to work, to pull off the linen cloths before they were soaked, but instead she sank to the ground and the smallest of the kittens climbed into her lap, turned in a circle, plopped down and began to methodically clean its face. The kitten's weight was comforting, and she allowed herself to close her eyes for just a moment.

A pulsing ache in her leg brought her out of the dream.

Someone stood over her, shining a bright light in her eyes. She tried to resist, to move her head to the right or left. Her heart rate accelerated and her mind searched for an explanation of what was happening. Still the person with the light persisted. Perhaps if she opened her eyes, just for a minute, the person would go away.

"There she is. That's good, Annie. I know it hurts."

Great. She'd done it! She squeezed her eyes shut, hoping the woman would go away.

"One more time for me. That's excellent."

"Could you…turn out the lights?"

Her voice was scratchy and her throat sore, but all that was nothing compared to the piercing pain in her head.

Why was she in a room with such bright lights?

Why wasn't she at home?

"Can we…" Her *mamm*'s voice calmed her rising panic, but her confusion only increased. Where was she? Why did her *mamm* sound as if she was at the end of a long tunnel?

"Could we please cut the lights?"

"Of course."

Someone jumped up, turned them off and Annie breathed a sigh of relief.

Her *mamm*'s face popped in front of her field of vision. She looked pale and tired and about to cry. "Oh, Annie."

And then her *dat* was there, patting her *mamm*'s shoulder and assuring them both that everything would be okay. She sensed more than saw that someone else was in the room, and then she looked past her *mamm*, past her *dat*, and saw

Levi. He offered a little wave. He looked as if he'd been crying too, and as if he hadn't slept in quite some time.

She wondered what had happened, why they all looked so bereft and relieved at the same time.

Where was she?

She glanced to the left of her bed, where a doctor was smiling and tapping something into a tablet computer. Looking back at her family, she asked, "What happened?"

Her *mamm* and *dat* and Levi all looked at one another, and seemed to silently come to the agreement that her *mamm* would be the one to tell her. "You don't remember?"

"*Nein*. Nothing."

"You were in a wreck. A truck hit you."

"Bella?" She tried to sit up, but it felt as if an invisible hand pushed her back. "Is Bella…"

"The horse is fine. You were in Priscilla's truck, pulling the wedding trailer."

And suddenly she did remember—the wedding, the conversation with Levi, leaving in the truck. Explaining to Priscilla how confused she was about her feelings.

"Priscilla?"

"She's *gut*." Her *mamm* smoothed the white hospital blanket. "She suffered a broken arm as well as some cuts and bruises. Her arm has already been set in a cast, and they released her the same day. She comes by every afternoon to check on you. We've all been…worried."

"How long have I been here?"

"The accident was three days ago. Christmas is tomorrow."

She looked past her *mamm* to Levi, who nodded, held her gaze.

"I'd like to check a few things, and then I'll answer any additional questions you have." The doctor placed the tablet on a small table. "If Dad and Boyfriend could give us a few minutes…"

Boyfriend? She still couldn't remember the accident at all, but there was one thing she knew for certain—Levi wasn't her boyfriend. Before she could protest, though, Levi glanced down at her leg which looked huge.

Was her leg in a cast?

Had she broken it?

And why couldn't she remember what had happened over the last three days?

"We'll be right outside," Levi assured her.

None of it made any sense.

She had so many questions. Before she could decide which one to ask first, the doctor—whose white coat was embroidered with the name Dr. Tallman—helped her sit up and told her to lean forward. She placed the cold stethoscope on her back and said, "Take a real deep breath for me."

Levi probably should have left when Annie's parents did, but he couldn't. He needed to be certain that she was okay. He needed to talk to her.

At first there had been too many people in the room. Confessing feelings for a girl wasn't something you could comfortably do in front of her parents. He wanted to talk to her, and he wanted to do it before going back to his room at Bishop Marcus's.

But was now even the right time?

Maybe he should wait. He hadn't told her at the wedding and then there had been the accident. *Nein.* He wouldn't put it off again. He wouldn't take that chance.

He didn't understand his feelings himself. How was he going to explain them to her? She might reject him. She probably would, but at this point he had to try.

Her parents had left when they'd brought in her dinner tray. She'd eaten four bites—he'd actually counted—and then fallen asleep. She'd been sleeping for three days straight. It seemed to him that she'd be all rested up. But as the doctor reminded them all, Annie had been through quite a shock and her injuries would take time to heal.

"Sleep is the best thing for her," Dr. Tallman had said more than once.

He'd wait all night if he had to. If they didn't kick him out. Priscilla stopped by after the abbreviated dinner, toting a ridiculously large teddy bear wearing a Christmas sweater. Levi stood out in the hall with her, watching nurses walk back and forth, families coming in for visitation, even a woman with a dog that wore a vest proclaiming the Labrador was a *Comfort Dog*.

"She seemed okay?" Priscilla adjusted the sling which cradled her broken arm. "You're sure?"

"*Ya.* When we told her about the accident, she asked about the horse and you…"

"She didn't remember being in my truck?"

"*Nein.* She didn't remember anything about the accident. I thought she'd be upset about the trailer, but she waved it off after reminding us it was insured."

Priscilla smiled—the first time he'd seen her do that since the accident. "Annie insisted that we have a business plan and do all this research. If you could have seen the books she brought home from the library…"

"Sounds like Annie."

"Of course I had auto insurance, and the loan we took out for the trailer required that we have insurance for it as well." She shook her head, resting her back against the wall and closing her eyes. "Annie insisted on business insurance—it covers the trailer, its contents and any gigs that we miss because of an accident."

"Wow."

"Yeah." She stood up straighter, opened her eyes and smiled.

"Doesn't sound very Amish. We usually go with *if it's Gotte's wille…*"

"Uh-huh. She told me that, but she also said most Amish folk didn't invest as much as we had in something that could be demolished by one teen texting while driving."

"Only it was a middle-aged male truck driver, not a teen."

"And it was a mechanical failure, not inattention."

They both thought about that for a moment. Levi was reminded again how the truck had hit Annie's side of the vehicle. She could have been killed. That thought ran through his mind constantly. She could have been, but she wasn't.

The fact that Priscilla had walked away relatively unhurt and Annie was mending rapidly truly was a miracle.

After watching Priscilla show up at the hospital every night, even staying the night of the accident though she was in obvious pain herself, he understood that they were more than business partners. They were friends and close ones at that.

"How did you two meet?"

"We took a cake-making class at the same time."

"Cake making?"

"Fancy cakes for big parties and important birthdays and anniversaries and weddings."

"You both took a class together?"

"At the library, yeah. I had this vague idea that I'd like to host parties for a living, and Annie—well, Annie already had a wedding business detailed in her little notebook."

He'd seen that notebook, the first day he'd been at her house.

"I've never been a great baker and taking that class confirmed as much. My cake fell so that there was this giant crater in the middle. My sugar roses looked like lumps of frosting. Annie started laughing and couldn't stop." She wiped at her eyes. "It didn't matter that she was Amish and I wasn't. We've been best friends from that first night."

"I understand."

"Do you?"

"Sure. Sometimes friendship surprises you. Sometimes it grows out of a relationship that you'd never have thought could become so close."

Priscilla studied him a minute. "Have you and Annie talked?"

"About what?"

"About how you feel?"

"How I feel?"

Now she laughed outright. He would have been offended if he hadn't been so surprised.

"Don't ask me how I know. It's as plain as the suspenders you're wearing."

"It is?"

"To me, anyway. To someone who knows Annie as well as I do. She talks about you all the time."

"She does?"

"Talk to her, Levi."

"We have—sort of."

"You've discussed your feelings?"

"Not really. I mean a little, but nothing personal. Her parents were in the room, and then the doctors and nurses are coming in and out constantly. So we've talked but not about my feelings—not really, no, we haven't."

She stood straighter and squeezed Levi's arm. "So why are you standing here? Go in there and wait for her to wake up and then say what you need to say."

"*Ya*, I plan to."

"Just do it." She pushed the teddy bear into his arms and adjusted the strap of her purse over her shoulder. "Oh, and when she does wake up, give her the bear. And tell her I'll be back tomorrow night. Tell her I'll bring the Scrabble board."

He watched her walk away, and then he went back into Annie's room.

Chapter Fourteen

The lights were low and the television was off. Come to think of it, the television hadn't been turned on as far as he knew. He settled into the chair that could be adjusted to form a small bed, though he didn't bother with that. Instead he covered himself with the blanket the nurses had kindly left, stared at the wall and tried to decide what he'd say when Annie finally woke.

An hour later, she tried to turn over in her sleep and let out a yelp.

He catapulted from the chair.

"You can't do that."

"Why?"

"Your leg…it's broken and in a splint."

"Oh."

"They're planning to put a cast on it tomorrow. The doctor said she was waiting for your swelling to go down, and then they didn't really want to move you around a lot until you were awake—if they didn't have to."

She stared at him a moment, then nodded and closed her eyes. He turned to go back to his chair, but she reached out and claimed his hand.

"Can I get you something?"

"A cup of water?"

"Sure, there's some right here." His hand shook as he poured water from the small pitcher into the cup. He showed her how to raise the head of the bed, and he made sure the straw was where she could reach it. Seeing her hand, still bandaged and sporting the IV, caused a lump to rise in his throat.

She handed the cup back to him. "Maybe pull a chair up closer."

"*Ya*, of course."

"Why are you holding a teddy bear?"

"This?" He hadn't realized he'd been holding it since she'd first yelped. "It's from Priscilla. She came by to see you."

He settled it in the bed beside her, even covered it up with the blanket, and was relieved to see a smile tug at the corners of her mouth.

"My parents didn't tell me everything. What were they holding back?"

He thought about that a minute. They'd answered all of her questions, but they had downplayed how much danger she'd been in. "I guess they didn't really describe how scared they were—how scared we all were. The bishop was here. Actually, the waiting room was filled with people from our district."

"I don't remember seeing any of them."

"The doctors weren't sure why you weren't waking up. None of their tests indicated a concussion. One doctor was worried that you'd slip into a coma, but then the other one—Dr. Tallman—said she'd seen this before and that your body just needed rest. She said that as long as your blood pressure and pulse were strong, to let you sleep."

"Three days?" She stared out the darkened window. "It's strange how you can lose a chunk of your life and never even realize it."

Levi didn't know how to answer that, so he didn't.

"You're sure Priscilla is okay?"

"*Ya*. She was here earlier. Brought the bear…" He cleared his throat—thinking of all she'd said. Thinking of her admonition for him to talk to Annie now, while there was time. Basically reminding him not to take anything for granted. As if he needed that reminder. "She said she'd be back tomorrow and that she'd bring the Scrabble board."

Annie nodded as if she expected as much. "How is the truck driver?"

"He didn't even have to go to the hospital."

"I wish I could remember."

You're better off not knowing, he thought.

But then he realized that he would want to know if it had happened to him—so he told her everything. He described hearing the crash, not understanding that it was Annie and Priscilla, leaving Petunia and the buggy in the middle of the road and running toward the tangle of cars in the intersection. When he reached the part about pushing his way through the crowd to her side, about the doctor who happened to be two cars back, his hands began to shake.

"It scared you," she said.

"Of course it did."

"Maybe it's one of those things that's worse to watch than it is to experience."

"Maybe."

"I'm not looking forward to dragging a cast around for the foreseeable future."

The splint on her leg was large and awkward. Levi realized it must be very difficult for her to get comfortable at all. "Do you need it moved or something?"

"*Ya*. Maybe a little."

So he moved it left, then right and then left again. He moved her leg as gently as if it had been a newborn baby. He was so afraid of hurting her, of making things worse. Was that why he hadn't talked to her of his feelings? Was he worried that doing so could make their relationship worse? But keeping it inside, well that wasn't going to work, either.

Finally Annie sighed and waved him back to the chair.

"I've never had a cast," Annie admitted. "It always looked like fun, when someone in school would have one and everyone would sign it."

"We're not in school, but I'll sign your cast."

Her eyebrows shot up, but she seemed to detect the underlying fear beneath his banter.

"Tell me the rest."

"I wish… I wish you could have seen Priscilla's truck. Maybe someone took pictures. I don't know. But if you'd seen it, how completely demolished it was, I think you'd be grateful for just a splinted leg or a cast. You both could have been killed."

She nodded as if she understood and maybe she did. She rubbed her temples, and he wondered if even sitting up was painful for her.

"Do you want me to call the nurse?"

"Nein."

"It's understandable if you'd like some pain medication—"

She shook her head as if to dispel his concern. Finally she turned her brown eyes toward him and pinned him to the spot with a look. "I'm tired of sleeping, but I'm still tired. Does that make sense?"

"Ya." He knew about that sort of weariness, only his had come from the problems with his family, from always looking for the next spot where he was sure he'd find peace and contentment, from trying to scratch the itch that was his broken dream.

"Why are you still here?"

"Excuse me?"

"Mamm and Dat went home. Priscilla came and left. Why are you still here?"

"I didn't want you to spend Christmas Eve alone." He glanced around the room. A volunteer had come by with a tiny Christmas tree, and another had brought some artificial holly that had been draped across a shelf. There were no gifts, none of the normal things they would equate with Christmas, but he knew that the next morning her family would bring gifts and handmade cards from the children.

"Have you been doing this every night?"

"Ya, but…"

"What's going on, Levi? What aren't you telling me?"

He realized he couldn't put it off any longer. He was terrified, nearly as afraid as he'd been as he ran toward the truck. But in that moment he understood that the only thing worse than being rejected by her would be never taking the chance, and so he stood, poured himself a cup of water and drained it. Finally he sat back down on the chair next to her bed.

He wasn't sure exactly how he was going to say it, but he knew that it was now or never.

Annie felt her pulse begin to beat more rapidly. Had the accident somehow damaged her heart? Was she about to pass out? But she somehow knew that what she was feeling had nothing to do with her physical condition. It was the way that Levi was looking at her that made her pulse race. It was something tickling her memory that was causing her hands to sweat. Something she couldn't quite pull to the front of her mind.

Levi finally put down the cup he was fiddling with and perched on the chair next to her bed.

"I've been struggling with this a while now. I can see that, and I'm tired of it. Tired of going to sleep wondering if it's just a crush, if tomorrow I'll wake up and feel differently."

"A crush?"

"Only it's not. Somehow I know it's not going to pass like a bad cold."

Did he just compare his feelings for her to a bad cold? She wanted to laugh. She wanted to grab his big shoulders and shake him. But what she wanted most was for him to look at her and say what he meant.

"How I feel about you—it isn't going away. I guess I've known that for a while now."

His eyes met hers, and suddenly she remembered the kiss they'd shared, the way her heart had soared and her stomach had dropped, the certainty of her emotions when she'd confessed her feelings to Priscilla.

"I definitely never thought we'd be friends." She plucked at the blanket. "You and that ridiculous cowboy hat and boots and stories of Texas."

"We are *freinden* now." He smiled at her. "I guess neither of us saw that coming."

"I wasn't very kind when you first came to Goshen. I was so afraid of your dream, of your certainty that life would be better somewhere else. For some reason I'm not afraid of that anymore."

"I'm persuasive in that way." He gulped so hard that she saw his Adam's apple bob. "Or maybe *Gotte* has been the one doing the persuading, working on both of our hearts."

He reached for her hand and traced a finger down the inside of her palm causing goose bumps to pepper her skin.

"But what I'm feeling…" He cleared his throat and tried again. "It's more than friendship and it's more than a crush."

"It is?"

"How I feel about you, Annie, it's different than I've ever felt about anyone else."

"It is?"

"And what I want, what I dream of, is our being more to each other. I'm not satisfied with being your friend. I don't want to play it safe anymore. I'm ready to take a chance."

She shook her head, reached for her *kapp* strings and then realized she wasn't wearing one. Brushing back her hair, she met his gaze. "You're ready to take a chance on what? Levi, maybe it's my head injury, but I need you to speak more plainly."

"I want to close the distance between us. I want to be the other half of you—like two pieces of a puzzle that fit perfectly together."

"Are you saying you love me?"

"Yes. Annie Kauffmann, I love you." His gaze held steady, and she found that she had to look away. It was what she'd wanted to hear, what she'd told Priscilla that he was afraid of. Only now he wasn't. Now he was sitting here confessing his love after sitting by her side for three days.

"You're sure? Because after our kiss you said…"

"I said I was desperate. I was scared. I'll admit that." He stared at the floor a minute, then sat back and allowed a silence to settle over them. Finally he cleared his throat and chuckled.

"I was talking to Jebediah when he came up to check on you. I guess he helped me to see what should have been obvious."

"My *bruder*?"

"*Ya*. He asked me how I felt when we're apart. He asked me, did I miss hanging out or did I miss your face, your touch, your laugh."

"I never knew my *bruder* was such a romantic."

"He said there's a difference between wondering what's going on in your life and needing to know how your day was. There's a difference between caring about you and wanting—*nein*, needing to spend the rest of our lives together."

Annie nodded, a lump forming in her throat, wishing he would stop because she was about to cry, and praying that he wouldn't stop because she wanted to hear…to finally hear what was in his heart.

"And then I realized there's a difference between loving someone like a *schweschder* in Christ, like a family member or a friend, and loving someone so much that you feel a little sick in your stomach."

"Like you have a bad cold."

"Exactly." He grinned and she was reminded of that first night, of him following her out to the wedding trailer and rambling on about Texas. "There's a difference in loving someone in a general sense, and needing to say the words *I love you*. I do love you, Annie, and if you feel the same…"

"I do." The words slipped from her lips as simply as rain falling to the ground, and suddenly the weight on her heart was gone. Just like that. The burden of her love for him, it was lighter because she'd shared it. Why had she waited so long to tell him?

"You do?"

"*Ya*. I think I have for some time now."

"Why didn't you say something?"

She shrugged and remembered suddenly all that stood between them. She remembered afresh the grief at realizing she could have her dream of a successful wedding business or she could have Levi—but it didn't seem that she could have both.

Tears slipped down her cheeks and she brushed them away. "It's just that I didn't see how…how we could make it work."

"Why, Annie? Tell me why." When she didn't answer, he pushed a little harder. "Is it because of Texas?"

"Yes and no."

"Maybe I'm the one with the head injury now, but I need you to explain it to me."

"I don't want to move. I don't think I want to

move. I'm willing to admit that I'm terrified of that possibility. I love you, Levi, but I also love what I have here, my business with Priscilla. It's more than just a job."

"I know it is."

"We make a real difference in people's families. We help them to celebrate one of the most important days of their lives. It's a real blessing to do that."

"I understand."

"Do you?"

"Yes, and I'm willing to stay in Goshen."

"You are?"

"If that's what it takes? Then I'll stay. We'll live here, and we'll make it work."

"But I can't do that." Now she rubbed a fist against her chest. It was all coming back. Confessing her feelings to Priscilla, looking up and seeing the truck sail through the light, the split second when she knew they were about to be hit, wondering if that was it—if her life was going to end before she'd known the love of a husband, or the joy of children or the satisfaction of caring for a family.

"I can't do that to you. I don't understand why *Gotte* put Texas in your heart, but I understand that he did. You wouldn't be...wouldn't be the man I know, the man I love, without that ridiculous hat or those silly boots."

"You like my boots?" His voice was soft and teasing. The expression in his eyes was anything but.

Had anyone ever loved her as much as he did?

Had anyone ever looked at her that way before? She didn't think so, and the realization of it took her breath away.

"I want to put my arms around you," he whispered.

"But you can't." The tears were falling like a cleansing rain now. "I'm all hooked up." She raised her arm with the IV drip as proof.

He settled for reclaiming her hand between both of his.

"Annie, I don't know the solution to where we'll live or how or when. I'm not going to lie to you and tell you that I have any of those answers."

"That's not what I want. I don't want you to lie to me just so I'll feel better."

"The thing is that you're more important to me than Texas. You're more important to me than any dream I had before I met you. *Gotte* replaced that desire of my heart with a better one—something true and lasting."

"But you'll always resent me if we stay here."

"I won't. That's the miraculous thing, because Texas without you…well, it wouldn't be worth having." He scooted forward and thumbed the tears from her face. "Do you believe me?"

"*Ya.* I do."

"So will you?"

"Will I what?"

"Will you marry me, Annie Kauffmann? I can't imagine a better Christmas gift than your saying yes."

"I made you a wool scarf."

"Did you now?"

"It's blue, like the wildflowers in Texas."

"Which reminds me of something." He jumped up, retrieved his coat, and handed her a snow globe.

She shook it, gazed at the bluebonnets and the snow, thought of Christmas and what did and didn't make it perfect. It was the people in your life that mattered. It was having those that loved you near, and it didn't really matter what state you lived in, only that you were there for one another.

She shook it again and then raised her eyes to meet his. "It's beautiful."

"You're beautiful."

"Have you been carrying this around in your pocket?"

"Jebediah fetched it from my place. I wanted to have it here, for when you woke up. I wanted to make you smile at Christmas."

The tears began to slip down her cheeks.

"Will you be my bride and have my children and share my dreams and trials and all of my tomorrows?"

"I will."

"Then the rest we'll figure out." He stood, leaned over her bed and kissed her softly on the lips.

The ache in her chest disappeared.

The tears stopped.

The fear she'd been harboring evaporated.

And all that was left was the certainty that whatever they faced in the future, wherever they faced it, they'd do so together.

Epilogue

Three years later

Annie picked Eli up out of his crib and carried him to the front porch. An east wind was blowing, cooling the Texas afternoon. She sat in the rocker and watched Levi walk across the field toward home.

He bounded up the front porch steps, kissed her on the lips and then kissed the top of Eli's head.

"Did he just wake up?"

"He did."

"So he probably won't go down until late."

"He probably won't."

"Which means we won't be going to bed until late."

"Exactly."

Levi pulled off his hat, an Amish hat made of straw with a wide brim. He dropped it on the porch floor and ran his hands through his hair. She'd need to cut it again soon. It was already tickling his collar.

"I suppose that'll give me another chance to beat you at Scrabble."

"You wish."

He went into their house and fetched two glasses of lemonade. She should have thought of that, but the truth was, she'd slept while Eli had slept, and she wasn't fully awake yet. The doctor had said her tiredness was completely normal given the twins she was carrying.

"I spoke with Jebediah today."

"Ya?"

"He said he's going into Hamilton tomorrow for the animal auction. Believe it or not he wants to buy a colt for his son."

"Joshua is hardly old enough for that."

"So I told him." Levi grinned at her. "He asked if I wanted to go along."

"And do you?"

"Of course. Your older *bruder* is going to need a buggy horse."

Slowly her entire family was moving to Texas. They'd settled on the same land that Levi had first scouted—the land that had belonged to Betty and Buddy Johnston. Dry-land farming was difficult, even more difficult than in Indiana, but they were making it. Her parents had been with the first group that moved. She and Levi had moved with the second group, though he'd put his deposit down on a portion of Buddy's land. Profits from her wedding business had helped to pay off the loan.

They hadn't moved as soon as they'd married, partly because Annie had been pregnant with Eli by that time. Instead they'd waited, corresponded regularly with the dozen families who had set up the community, and prayed about what to do next.

Eighteen months ago they'd made the move. The new community wasn't so small anymore. It had grown to nearly twenty families—families that were adding little ones regularly. By the time Eli was a grown man, *Gotte* willing, they'd be ready to split into two districts.

For now, they were still small enough that they didn't need a wedding trailer, not yet. But she wrote to Priscilla every week. Her friend would be moving to Texas in a few months, and they had plans to start a smaller catering business that included an Amish bakery the following spring.

The sun dropped farther down the wide expanse of Texas sky, sending out bands of pink and purple and lavender.

"It's beautiful," Levi said.

"*Ya*, it's as *gut* as you described back when you were trying to convince us to come to Texas."

Levi laughed, drained his glass and placed it

on the wooden crate between them. He stood and walked over to her rocker—stopped behind it and placed his hands on her shoulders, leaned down to whisper in her ear.

"I wasn't talking about the view."

"You weren't?"

"Or the sunset."

"It is beautiful, though."

"I was talking about you." He kissed her cheek, then said softly, "Stay where you are. Supper can wait. I'll take this little one and go clean us both up."

As he walked into the house, she did what he said.

Dinner could wait.

She could hear Eli talking in his baby language to Levi.

She placed her hands on the mound that used to be her stomach. "Promise me you won't ride in the rodeo," she said to the babies. She'd been to see several, and she couldn't imagine letting any boy of hers ride a bull, or any girl of hers chase lambs. She wanted to keep them safe. She wanted to protect them against anything and everything.

Of course that wasn't her job to do. *Gotte* would do that, the same way He'd kept her safe during the accident, the same way He'd brought her and Levi together.

She sat in the rocker, watching the first of

the stars make their appearance, and realized—again—just how happy she was. She didn't have to worry about whether her oldest *bruder* would like Texas as much as they did, or if it would rain the next week. She could do her best each day and that was enough—which at the moment meant sitting on the front porch rocking and soaking in the blessings of her life.

* * * * *

If you loved this story,
pick up the other books in the
Indiana Amish Brides series,

A Widow's Hope
Amish Christmas Memories
A Perfect Amish Match

from bestselling author
Vannetta Chapman

Available now from Love Inspired!
Find more great reads at
www.LoveInspired.com

Dear Reader,

Have you ever cherished a dream in your heart—
something that was so important to you that you
viewed everything else through the lens of what
you hoped would happen? A dream can be a wonderful thing. But what about when our dreams
blind us to the path in front of us? What happens
when the things we are convinced should happen, don't?

Annie Kauffmann believes she is happy helping other people's dreams come true. She's a
nurturer, a hard worker and a kind person. She's
settled for a far different dream than she once
had—when she believed that she would find
true love, marry a kind man and raise a family.
Now she's convinced that while God grants those
things for other people, for her, life has taken a
different path. She focuses on her work, on making others happy, on finding financial security.

Levi Lapp is pursuing the dream that he has
held close since he was a young child when life
was simple and good, before he learned that not
everyone could be trusted. Before he had his heart
broken not by romantic love but by those adults
who were supposed to guide him into adulthood.
He longs to find his way back to a time when he
still held hope and optimism about the future, and

he's convinced the way to do that is to go back to the physical place where he experienced the happiest years of his youth.

Annie and Levi are so busy pursuing what they are sure will make them happy, that they almost miss the blessings God has laid out for them.

I hope you enjoyed reading this book. I welcome comments and letters at *vannettachapman@gmail.com*.

May we continue to always give thanks to God the Father for everything, in the name of our Lord Jesus Christ (Ephesians 5:20).

Blessings,
Vannetta

Get 4 **FREE REWARDS!**

We'll send you 2 FREE Books <u>plus</u> 2 FREE Mystery Gifts.

Love Inspired® Suspense books feature Christian characters facing challenges to their faith... and lives.

FREE Value Over **$20**

Get 4 FREE REWARDS!

We'll send you 2 FREE Books plus 2 FREE Mystery Gifts.

Harlequin® Heartwarming™ Larger-Print books feature traditional values of home, family, community and—most of all—love.

FREE Value Over $20

THE FORTUNES OF TEXAS COLLECTION!

18 FREE BOOKS in all!

Treat yourself to the rich legacy of the Fortune and Mendoza clans in this remarkable 50-book collection. This collection is packed with cowboys, tycoons and Texas-sized romances!

YES! Please send me **The Fortunes of Texas Collection** in Larger Print. This collection begins with 3 FREE books and 2 FREE gifts in the first shipment. Along with my 3 free books, I'll also get the next 4 books from The Fortunes of Texas Collection, in LARGER PRINT, which I may either return and owe nothing, or keep for the low price of $5.24 U.S./$5.89 CDN each plus $2.99 for shipping and handling per shipment*. If I decide to continue, about once a month for 8 months I will get 6 or 7 more books but will only need to pay for 4. That means 2 or 3 books in every shipment will be FREE! If I decide to keep the entire collection, I'll have paid for only 32 books because 18 books are FREE! I understand that accepting the 3 free books and gifts places me under no obligation to buy anything. I can always return a shipment and cancel at any time. My free books and gifts are mine to keep no matter what I decide.

☐ 269 HCN 4622   ☐ 469 HCN 4622

Name (please print)

Address   Apt. #

City   State/Province   Zip/Postal Code

Mail to the **Reader Service:**
IN U.S.A.: P.O. Box 1341, Buffalo, N.Y. 14240-8531
IN CANADA: P.O. Box 603, Fort Erie, Ontario L2A 5X3